ESPERANZA

KARIM FADALI

iUniverse, Inc.
New York   Bloomington

Esperanza

This is a work of fiction. All of the characters, names, incidents, organizations, and dialogue in this novel are either the products of the author's imagination or are used fictitiously.

iUniverse books may be ordered through booksellers or by contacting:

iUniverse
1663 Liberty Drive
Bloomington, IN 47403
www.iuniverse.com
1-800-Authors (1-800-288-4677)

Because of the dynamic nature of the Internet, any Web addresses or links contained in this book may have changed since publication and may no longer be valid. The views expressed in this work are solely those of the author and do not necessarily reflect the views of the publisher, and the publisher hereby disclaims any responsibility for them.

ISBN: 978-1-4401-8467-3 (pbk)
ISBN: 978-1-4401-8468-0 (ebk)

Printed in the United States of America

iUniverse rev. date: 10/26/2009

Take a deep breath, let go of what you know and believe. Let go and step with me into a rural marketplace set over brown soil, at the foot of the winding Atlas Valley.

Walk past colorfully dressed Berber women, squatting or sitting crossed legged next to spread out tarps covered with freshly harvested vegetables, round trays holding heaps of rich local spices, cooking pots, frying pans and second-hand clothes.

Join the crowd of standing farmers, young and old, children and women, and, listen to a wrinkled old fellow who is calmly standing at the center of the human circle, just as he begins laying the background of our story...

"I heard it said, from a saddened heart that somewhere on the southern coast of Andalusia sits a fishing village where every man is born a sailor and every woman, a potential widow.

"I heard it whispered, like a lament, that it is a very quiet and dull place -much avoided by the passing yachts with whatever riches and affluence they happen to carry within; for even from the furthest distances, this village is nothing more than a desolate arrangement of overlapping shadows and pale blocks, its mere sighting affecting unpleasant shutters and undeniable feelings of anguish and loss.

"Imagine an uninviting patch of land, permeated and insulated by the weight of its own history, cloaked with gloom, unscathed by the swaying of seasons and national moods, by the passing wars, the taste and smell of gun powder, an isolated island in a sea of change, forgotten by time and development.

"Imagine unexplainable silence, suffusing the air, brooding and bone chilling, and that is exactly the way this land appeared to anyone who didn't belong there… but not anymore. No, not anymore, or to be more accurate, not since a few years back when the tallest and widest wall facing the sea from the eastern flank of this village was made into a larger than life painting.

"I am talking about a painting unlike any other, a painting that was born in strangeness, a mystery within a mystery, an unexpected sight that was, within days of its apparition, strongly denounced by the local clergy, condemned by the church, but always, protected by the villagers.

"Imagine. These were peaceful people, who knew the meaning of hardship, modesty and frugality. They were toiling folks who had no room for trouble and nonsense. They had not asked for this mural to be painted. Yet, they stood up, unflinching against the pressuring demands of affluent clergymen, to keep her from being erased, from that wall and out of their lives, and to anyone who tries to argue against their illogical decision, they, to this day, raise their hands and say, 'she was meant to come.'

"They say, 'she is one of us —always has been,' before asking, 'How could we go against one of our own? How could we go against her?' 'No, we could never do that.' Then and finally, admiring the beautiful young woman with unsettling hazel eyes, in a white summer dress, hovering over a carpet of green grass, her feet almost brushing the ground, forever carried, and lifted by a gentle breeze, they state, as if it were enough to explain everything, 'She is Esperanza.'

"Even now, if you were to go there, and could wait long enough, you too would hear them whisper, calling her name, 'Esperanza.' And if you were to ask, 'Who is this Esperanza?' They would simply smile and reply, 'She is our sister. She is the daughter of winds. She is the light we seek in our darkness days.'

"Brothers and sisters, boys and girls, to you I say this: Don't be surprised if you begin dreaming of her, because she is said to be sought by those with broken hearts and lost dreams. To this very moment, and from the time of her blessed birth, word has been traveling, around the country and even beyond, that who ever lays eyes on her will find peace of mind. So, don't be surprised if one day you find yourself in that village, in front of that wall, shedding tears from your heart… Yes, don't be surprised the day you meet Esperanza."

Gently a soft breeze moves through the valley and the marketplace, like a paintbrush, erasing sky, hills, dirt, trees, grass, the old man, the crowd you've joined, the vendors with all of their merchandises and everyone else that was there, replacing your surroundings with the darkness of late night hours. You begin feeling light, and realize that you have become a shadow floating among others.

You're in the living room of an apartment you don't recognize. You begin moving along the walls, exploring the place. You find a kitchen, sparkling clean and well organized, then a bathroom that smells of jasmine blossoms and where everything is where it ought to be. You float through a short hallway and see two doors. You slip underneath one of them and find an unoccupied room furnished with a large uncluttered desk, a pair of office chairs, sturdy looking bookshelves and a couple of wide file cabinets. You take it all in, and, get back to the hallway.

There, inspired by the night and its hidden secrets, unburdened by any feeling of haste or fear, you pause and listen for clues in the surrounding silence. Then, through the open gap between floorboard and door, you enter the second room, a bedroom where a man and a woman happen to be lying still, each on one side of the king size mattress they are sharing.

Four o'clock in the morning, she lies awake, eyes wide open, staring at the ceiling. The room feels cold, yet she prefers to remain uncovered. Next to her, completely wrapped and shrouded in a blanket, Adil, her husband, is lost in deep slumber. She knows he is there, yet she feels alone, totally alone.

In a few hours, and just as she has been doing every day for the last couple of years now, she'll sit up very carefully, put on her slippers, walk to the bathroom, slide out of her night gown, step into the bathtub, and under the shower head. She will let water, warm to the touch, hit her face, before running down the rest of her dead epidermis, and finally spiraling into oblivion, washing along a stream of tears and sorrow.

Her name is Yasmine Berrada. She was born thirty years ago in the heart of Fez, the cultural and historic pearl of North Africa. However, it is in Casablanca, the largest and liveliest Moroccan city that she was raised. Her family had moved to the country's business capital, in order for her father, Anouar Berrada —May God rest his soul (as those who knew or had simply heard of him tended to say when his name was mentioned), a promising political figure, to secure his first leading position in the Ministry of Finance. It is also in Casablanca that Yasmine obtained a degree in law, became a respected attorney, and met Adil.

Their first encounter had happened on an evening she could still vividly remember. Adil had arrived at her home, where he had been invited for dinner by her mother, Amina —or Lalla Amina, as the sophisticated woman insisted on being called, for the respect the matriarchal title entailed.

Yasmine was standing at a staircase, a long hallway separating her from Lalla Amina and her guests. She had heard about them, many times throughout the days that had led to this one. She had learnt about them, in measured increments, from the scheming woman who gave her birth, the woman who wanted nothing but the very best for her baby.

She glanced at her latest suitor, and found nothing but a dull figure, an awkward fellow trying to look his best, trying too hard. She was well acquainted with his kind: Fools on a mission, shopping for brides to impregnate, dominate and humiliate time and time again. She felt her stomach churn with anger; anger towards him, but mainly towards her mother, because, it was her mother's doing -as usual. Lalla Amina had once again found a prospective groom for her, and just like all the others that had come before him, he was just another male in a man's world, born into the natural vanity of his gender, raised to believe himself righteously superior to every woman, except his mother.

Yasmine wished the one she loved were standing there instead, for only to him could she give herself –and hadn't she already. Unfortunately, that, along with their love, had to remain a secret, sealed in discretion, at least until the time was ripe. Gritting her teeth, she cursed money, and people who couldn't see past it, people like her parents, for whom how much one had was more important than the making of one's character, rendering honor and decency of heart completely irrelevant if they were not backed by immeasurable wealth. Bitterly smiling for the guests, she cursed money, or its lack there of, for standing, like an insurmountable obstacle between her heart and true happiness.

Yasmine cursed money and those who had it, like this character who was mindlessly ogling at her –and what else did he have to offer anyway? She met his eyes with a gaze she hoped would subtly convey all the contempt she was feeling toward his kind. It was all she could do, so as not to suffer one of her mother's moral sermons. The last thing she needed was being chastised because of her unacceptably childish behavior, lack of maturity and ut-ter disrespect for her family's name and reputation. She knew from experience, that there would be no end to it. The finger pointing would go on for days, and there would be no escape from the reprimanding bouts of a grieved mother who, in the end, as she herself insists on putting it, wants nothing but her daughter's happiness.

However, while eyeing this prospective candidate with unspoken distaste, she somehow noticed his smile, shy and nervous, filled with all kinds of weaknesses, and almost immediately felt pity for the lad. Suddenly, she found herself wondering if she wasn't being too critical, too quick at judging someone about whom she actually didn't know much. After all, she reminded herself, he was nothing but a stranger. Yet, the well-behaved trophy-bride she was supposed to act as could not deny the raw feelings that had flooded her whole as soon as she laid eyes on him. No, and after second thought, she just could not help but despise him.

Meanwhile, her mother was speaking, being too charming a hostess. Undoubtedly, she was seeing in Adil the promise of a great future. Her smile was too wide, her laughter too sweet… and why not? Wasn't he, after all, as she had been hoping, and as Yasmine would soon come to appreciate, from a well-to-do and socially respected family? Not to forget the impressive fact that this young man of spotless upbringing had, already at thirty years of age, opened his own medical practice in the center of bustling Casablanca.

'But as the saying warns,' thought Yasmine as she moved down the stairs, 'Don't buy or sell fish while it's still darting freely in the water.' She still had to agree to the life binding proposition that farce of a man had brought along. She held herself from laughing gingerly, as she reflected, 'not only do I have to agree to be taken by this breathing nuisance, but so does my father, and Father, being the man he is, Minister of Finance, elegance and prestige in the flesh -the vainest of them all- he would never allow his own flesh and blood, his only daughter to be handed to such a spineless creature.'

Setting foot on the corridor's marbled floor, she allowed a muffled sigh to escape from her lips. She wished that he who was in charge of her family, as well as of the finances of the whole country was home. However, that was not to be, for the schedule of a minister is unlike that of most other heads of households. As was usually the case, her father was bound to be found traveling throughout the land, inaugurating this project, blessing that merging, meeting with all sorts of foreign investors in exclusive resorts, following His Majesty -The beloved king, head bowed, while waxing lyrical and praising his Blessed Highness to no end, hungry for power, always more power.

Three months later, the unthinkable happened, and that despite the minister's strong reluctance at seeing his name connected to that of mere peasants, country folk, uneducated Berbers from whom there was nothing to be gained, but shame and mediocrity, when on the other hand, there were decent Fassi bachelors whose name if added to theirs would not only bring great distinction, but would also assist him in moving forward in his quest at broadening his influence. The minister lavished at the idea of greater influence.

"Yes," his voice boomed with great enthusiasm, "What you should look for is influence where influence truly matters, through a well-formed association with a son of a great man, a heir to some visionary with assets in one, or why not, a couple of, tomorrow's industries, a leader in charge of the textile or technology industries, not sheep, not cows, not manure."

A stubborn man, he went on protesting, over and again, to a wife who could not see eye to eye with him when it came to Adil and his family, "They are in the sheep business," raising his hands in the air, adding, "The sheep business!" as if that last statement were enough to support his position in the matter. Meanwhile, Lalla Amina, not lacking in stubbornness herself, insisted on repeating over and over again, her pleas bracketed by generous displays of heartfelt sighs, if not tears streaming in the most dramatic of ways down her rosy flushed face, and let us not forget a sadness that seemed to be radiating from her every pore, "He would be such a good husband for our Yasmine, why won't you trust me? Why do you want to ruin your daughter's life? I don't understand. What has she done to you? Tell me. Tell me."

For over a week, the minister of Finance tried to make his case, but Lalla Amina wouldn't have any of it. She would start sobbing and sobbing. Being the seasoned politician that he was, he would just wait for her to stop and then repeat what he'd said one more time, and so their dance around the subject of Yasmine's future went on for days, and then weeks, without ever stopping to inquire what it was that Yasmine wanted.

Three months later, and unavoidably, considering all the plotting and scheming Lalla Amina had put into the matter, although there was more –reasons that could not be revealed yet- than a resourceful mother's pushing behind what finally took place, Yasmine Berrada and Adil Khadir were joined in Holy Matrimony, in strict adherence to the Islamic tradition, under both the law of the land and that of God, as father and groom shook hands and signed the legal registry.

A few days afterwards, their union was commemorated with a wedding so large and festive it was declared, by some experts in such events, to be the biggest and most phenomenal wedding of the year, which was to be expected as a fortune was spent and no effort was spared in order to impress the throngs of guests who had been invited to the celebration.

That night, in the Berrada's villa, the air, richly flavored with festive music mixed to the sweet amalgam of intoxicating spices, was affecting the general mood, while dish after dish, gigantic trays of sweet nutty pastries of all kinds and shapes, perfectly prepared chicken, lamb and fish, and more of the same, along with mountains of freshly baked breads, tea glasses and cool carbonated drinks, continued to flow, served by agile and smiling tuxedo-wearing professional banquet waiters hired to attend to the ravenous crowds.

On one side of the gathering, there were groomed men, covered as they were, and as such occasions required, in expensive suits, gold watches and easily recognizable imported cologne, mingled with skill, laughing generously, dipping small and large pieces of bread in succulent sauces, chewing pleasantly, swallowing with delectation and licking their fingers while nodding their heads approvingly and appreciatively for all the pleasures wealth can buy.

Then on the other, dressed to stand out and impress, in traditional handmade (one thread at a time) kaftans, long colorful dresses, scintillating like a thousand constellations on a clear summer night sky, displaying ageless artistic embroideries threaded with gold, on rare Indian silks, swam the charming women who lived to mingle. Freely, they laughed, kissed and hugged.

A few were dancing, others singing, celebrating this blessed union with utmost openness and genuineness. Meanwhile, and as in every other wedding, others hovered and merged into small clusters of familiarity, within which their scrutinizing hawkish eyes were bound to meet, before they lashed out -fully embodying the mythical snake that lies in the darkest crevice of the soul- into the worst and best kind of gossiping.

Whispering words coated with bitter sugar dipped in lyrical venom, they criticized, pointed out the most unforgivable flaws, revealing, one smirk at a time, every display of obvious lack of taste, shared secrets not meant to be heard -secrets that were dearest to others, and finally commented with expertise on the ongoing wedding. In doing so, they were acting the way their mothers, and their mothers' mothers had done before them, and if the Almighty allows it, the way their own daughters and granddaughters shall act as well.

Thus in the loom of time, but unbeknownst to them, they were holding the thread of some unspoken ritual, here, taut within a fleeting moment, a moment that stretched between past and future, a moment in which they adhered to every rule of propriety and consideration laid upon their heads, bowing to the cutting edge of 'Tradition's sword,' surrendering to this unfaltering guardian of honor and morality as it stood firmly rooted in a time lost to history itself.

Nevertheless, and regardless of whether these collective actions were perpetrated consciously or unconsciously, it was definitely that opportunity to gossip and criticize in the most festive of environments they enjoyed the most, and consequently, it was also one of the main reasons, along with the desire to socialize and eat sense-intoxicating-and-mind-blowing dishes, behind the long hours spent in preparation, when in front of mirrors they had applied, with utmost precision, layers upon layers of mascara, eye liner and lipstick, fading one color into another, emphasizing this and concealing that, before running, in a maddening frenzy, almost crushing anything or anyone obstructing their advance toward visual perfection, to the manicure-pedicure appointment, and finally, and rather inescapably, to that hard-to-book hair styling session from which they would always emerge ready for an excitingly awaited evening among friends and foes.

Such occasions as this one, were also naturally the best to display any jewels their families ever owned along with

– if they happen to be married- their dutiful husbands, their honors' protectors, their virtues' keepers, their financial providers, and at times -although a very minor detail in such circles- their love-mates, for even, in such superficiality, the presence of love, no matter how infinitesimal could not be denied –not that, out of those present, too many, if any, were to care about or even notice the lack of an emotion as impalpable and as debatable as love.

Consequentially, occupied by this and that, no one had been able to notice, or even intuit, how fake Yasmine's smile was, how broken her heart was, how inappropriate every glimmering light, musical note, glowing face, uncontained laughter, warm handshake, tearful prayer and sincere wish was. No, no one, not even Adil, seemed to care to see or know how the bride felt.

The charade simply went on, to everyone else's satisfaction, saving the best or worst –depending on whom you asked- for last, as at a culminating point, a cheerful crowd gathered awaiting with great exhilaration, the opening of a door, out of which a man's hand, in this case Adil's, was supposed to appear holding out, for the world to see, a reddened piece of feminine undergarment, proof of the bride's honorable upbringing and conduct, as well as, of the Berrada's outstanding morals, values and reputation.

That being the tradition, and the performance that could not be altered in order for the celebration to end, or even have any validity, what was supposed to happen happened, as in due time, a stained piece of underwear appeared and was tossed with a flourish of an honorable man's hand. Thus, the stained fabric floated in the air, unaware of its ascribed weight, indifferent to its short-lived importance, describing an almost magical arc through space, cheered on by the crowd, in joy and well hidden relief.

Unfortunately for those directly affected, as that night was no more than a stage where tradition was just a show of glitter and spotlights, decorum devoid of heart. Truth, given no space to be revealed, remained hidden behind the door, in a room infused with awkwardness. The bride with a law degree, and an already recognizable as well as reputable name, sat on the edge of a brand new (purchased for the occasion) bed, tears flowing down her face, carving a path on her cheeks before landing one drop at a time on her white wedding dress, at the center of a widening dark stain. She had just watched a man for whom she felt nothing pour, from a small plastic bottle, red blood collected from a slaughtered lamb, over a piece of undergarment purchased exclusively to be thrown out through a cracked open door, out of which his hand had slipped and then reappeared, followed by the most joyful of cheers, the culmination of a hypocritical ritual, played up in the most traditional of ways, in the most demeaning of ways.

Isolated from the rest of the world in that room, the couple waited for the noise to fade and the crowd to disperse. Isolated from each other by their own respective thoughts, they remained in darkness, him on one side of the bed and her still on the other. She hadn't stopped crying, and words had yet to be exchanged. He lit a cigarette, drew in nicotine and relaxed as smoke escaped through his nostrils and mouth. He was staring at her silhouette and felling the urge to say something that would make things easier, a few caring words that may brush away the thick cloud of awkwardness that somehow filled the whole room. He opened his mouth but no sound came out.

She was staring vaguely at the other side of the room, keeping her eyes away from the man she had just been wedded to, wishing she were somewhere else, far away from him, far away from her own disillusioned self. She was already regretting her choice, when she heard him say, "Stop crying, will you? No one will ever know... and I really don't care."

His voice reached Yasmine's guts, stinging with unspoken nuances, nauseating, stirring beastly anger as it passed. Seething within, she didn't respond but stopped crying. He sighed, wanting to add, "It's not like you're a whore or anything of the sort," instead he reached for the light switch, flipped it off, took off his shoes and stretched out on his side of the bed with the burning cigarette still between his dry lips.

Separated by silence and darkness, she was withdrawing into some freshly discovered inner recesses, dissolving into a darkness tasting of loathing and hatred. Meanwhile Adil, feeling lost in solitude and disappointment, focused on the lively flame throbbing at the tip of his Marlboro Light. This was a night neither of them would ever forget.

Adil Khadir was born in a village, somewhere in the Atlas valley, to an undoubtedly rich Berber family (whose pastoral ancestors once ruled Northern Africa from the Atlantic coast all the way to what time and wars turned to a country named Libya), owners of vast lands along with millions of sheep and an almost bottomless fortune. However, it was in Casablanca that he grew up. And it was also there that, through obsessive hard work and sheer determination, he became a doctor and, by the same token, the first member of the Khadir family to reach such elevated heights in the strenuously sloping path of knowledge.

Unfortunately, and since anything worth anything has to come with a price, Adil had, on his way to taking Hippocrates's oath, omitted to enjoy life, indulge in whatever it was his peers indulged in, be a kid like the rest of his siblings -six brothers and three sisters of whom he was the eldest.

Somehow, and many would say sadly, the only pleasure Adil cared for was the one he found in his father's satisfied glee while this father was reviewing his impressively studious son's test scores and school grades. Moreover, it was for that admiring, smiling and loving fatherly face that Adil had avoided any activity that would have distracted him from becoming a doctor. "What our country needs the most," he had heard his father explain to a friend of his, "is more doctors."

Adil never forgot those words. They guided him, as he struggled in order to please the man he adored the most, so much that, in the process, he managed to seclude himself from the world and all its uncertainties in the safety of scientific dogma, in the kingdom of knowledge's heart. He became a hermit of a figure isolated within a fortress built out of clever suppositions and verifiable facts, reinforced with experimental data, fortified with formulae and theorems, and defended with graphs and diagrams. Thus, he persevered until turning thirty-two, when he finally emerged out of his barricaded haven, as a solid, well-rounded cardiologist, who, when out of his subject of specialization, knew very, very little.

Doctor Khadir was clueless without his white coat, his stethoscope and all the electronic measuring equipment provided to his trade by modern ingenuity. He was lost especially when it came to women, whom, in general, he felt very attracted to, as well as very afraid of. Women, he believed, were too different, uncontrollable, unpredictably volatile, highly evolved, as if moving too close to the sun, surreally divine, unattainably tempting apparitions much like mirages or fleeting meteor showers. Yet, he dreamed of a respectful wife, with emerald eyes, long dark hair, a fair face, a generous bosom and hypnotically swaying hips, a partner with whom he would bring forth as many children as his father and mother had. This was, after all, the tradition of those from the Atlas valley. This was, most importantly, his way of emulating the father he so dearly idolized.

But as much as Adil needed to find a wife, he could not fathom finding one on his own. He knew too well how complicated pleasing his parents would be. He realized how much social status, names and reputations mattered. Most importantly, he was very aware of how disadvantaged he was, and had been ever since his conception, for no other reason than the name he bore —a name too disconnected from the city's respected upper class, and much too related to the countryside, to farming, to a world built around, and with, sheep, cows, goats, illiteracy, hard labor, and dirt.

As a doctor, and an excellent one with that, he had gone as far as he could considering the means he had had in hand, and considering the disadvantage of having a name such as Khadir, a name surely lacking in stature, prestige and recognition, a name with which one was bound to be limited in one's growth and success, bound to a very modest clientele from a struggling middle class. With such a name, in a world where families' origins and lineages supersede individual skill and prowess, the Berber doctor needed connections in higher social spheres, connections with names such as Benmanssour, Benjalloun, and Berrada, names resonating with culture, knowledge, history, and sophistication, names intrinsically linked to the history of that ancient city, adobe of culture and refinement, pearl of knowledge and art, that forever held the sweet name of Fez. Fortunately he was not alone. His mother was there to help him.

Luckily, Fatma, the illiterate, yet wiser than two theological scholars put together, woman of Berber origin and blood, knew of her son's weaknesses. The insightful mother of nine believed that for one to gain and receive one had to act. And since her son wouldn't, she decided to take matters into her own hands by seeking new friends and infiltrating private and highly selective circles of Fassi housewives whom she quickly learned to mimic, hiding her obvious lack of that accent peculiar to Fez, of refined taste, and of bourgeois sophistication, until she was able to gain their priceless trust and friendship.

Subtly, the cunning mother probed each of her new

acquaintances, in search of a suitable bride for her beloved son, whose age, profession, and fortune she skillfully flourished as bait whenever the situation proved opportune. Fatma hoped for a Fassi daughter-in-law, preferably stunningly beautiful, healthy, wealthy, clever, charming, well-mannered, respectful of traditions, honorable, and definitely -as this last requisite went without say- untouched by other men. Skillfully navigating the highest social strata of the big city, and with more ambition than she had known herself to possess until then, she was scouring for a jewel as precious as the one she had heard so much about, the one whose mother she hadn't met yet, the one named Yasmine Berrada.

Born into a life of harshness and hard work, Fatma was not the kind of woman inclined to giving up. On the contrary, like a seasoned predator closing in on its lunch, she knew how to wait and how to be unrelentingly diligent in her quest. Believing that life was rewarding to those who seek and act, she was not the least surprised when the time had come for her to reap the fruits of her patience and determination, as the day when Fatma and Lalla Amina were to meet arrived.

That day, the door of opportunity opened. Introductions were made, and a conversation followed. There were radiant smiles connected through the softness of laughter. There was praise and charm, balanced by unspoken words and subtly calculated verbal pauses. Above all, there was agreement carried through glances and looks of eyes where hidden agendas could be glimpsed glowing like distant stars. Yet, on that awaited day, Fatma, intoxicated by a tension that had arisen with the surfacing realization that she was standing, perhaps, at the very end of her search for the perfect princess, was failing to realize how much darkness, and how much hope Lalla Amina's smile was concealing.

Yasmine's mother knew very well that she had found the Arabian knight she has been wishing for her daughter. For what better husband than a young, already accomplished and still promising doctor? What better dowry than a purse as heavy as the Khadirs'? And moreover, what better time than now, before her troubled daughter gets too entangled with that worthless mischief she has been spending time with? The answers were clear, as clear as what had to be done. An invitation was proposed and, of course, accepted.

A few days later, at exactly the agreed upon time, Adil Khadir, accompanied by Lalla Fatma —as she would be referred to that night, arrived to the Berrada's door. Wearing brand new clothes, head swimming in doubt and expectation, face flushed and radiating heat, sweat sluicing down both underarms, and hands damp and cold, Adil rang the bell, and coughed a few times to clear his dry throat. Calmly, Lalla Fatma drew a white handkerchief from her purse and wiped his face while whispering a few soft words meant to calm him down. He tried to smile, but nervousness made him grimace instead.

Lalla Amina opened the door herself, presenting a bright and mostly affable smile to her guests. "Come in, come in," she said before giving each a warm and affectionate hug. "Welcome to my modest home," her voice was ringing with exhilaration as she lead them, into and through her mansion's garden—a visibly well cared for space where the scents of many fragrant flowers seemed to be mixing and mingling playfully in the air. Past that horticultural enclave -considered by many as clearly unrivaled in beauty and size within the confines of the large and prosperous metropolis —impressed mother and son, closely following their hostess, entered into a large white-walled two story building.

"This is your home," Lalla Amina offered with a modest voice as they stepped into a marbled hallway leading to a succession of living rooms, and, ending in front of a spiraling Victorian staircase on which Yasmine happened to be standing. It was the first time Adil laid eyes on Yasmine. She was talking to a maid, unaware of their presence. Her dark wavy hair was resting over her shoulders, lightly covering parts of her neck. "Oh, and there is my daughter," said Lalla Amina, pointing to the radiant figure at the end of the hallway. "Yasmine come here. Come, so I can introduce you to our guests."

It was right then and there, even before hello and how are you, that Adil fell, losing his mind, his sanity in Yasmine's heavenly profile around which everything else seemed to converge, dissolve and vanish. Forgetting to breathe, he watched her turn and start walking in his direction. Her natural grace caused him to shake from within. His legs were weakening with each labored breath his body took. He wished he could to loosen the tie that was strangling him. He wished he could run away, but knew he wouldn't be able to move, for her dismissive hazel eyes were cruelly tearing his world into pieces. He wanted to look away but his will was nowhere to be found. Even his pride was gone. He hoped no one would realize what was becoming of him. He closed his eyes, searching for strength, but the defiant eyes of this heavenly creature who seemed to be walking with the devil would no let go of him.

Yasmine claimed his thoughts from that moment on, and for the months that would follow, leaving him no other option but to ask for her hand, while strongly encouraged by both mothers. Painstakingly, he sought to win her heart while adhering to the prevailing Islamic rules of courtship. Carefully, he tried to impress her while avoiding any situation that might raise the slightest doubt about her or his honorable upbringing, always making a point of meeting with her in her family's home, or in reputable public establishments, in the company of a chaperon -her mother preferably.

As far as Doctor Khadir was concerned, there was

nothing else he could do but blindly desire her, even as she showed him nothing but cold and harsh disdain. Thus he suffered, humiliation after humiliation, until on a gloriously sunny Saturday morning, when out of the blue, she took him aside, to a corner of her home's garden, where absolutely no one else would be able to hear her, as she, without ever flinching and with dagger eyes, told him, unabashed, words he would never forget.

"You say you want to marry me. For months now, you've been coming to this house almost everyday, loaded with expensive gifts, and that permanently expecting and rather pathetic smile of yours. You court me as if I were…" she paused and looked up at the sky, brilliantly blue above their heads, before returning her penetrating gaze on him, and continuing, "as if I were the virgin you've been dreaming of and patiently awaiting. Is that what you really believe? Do you really think I'm a virgin? That I've never been touched? That I've been waiting for prince charming to come and snatch me from my miserable life? Do you?"

Adil didn't know how to answer. He stood there uncertain of what words to choose. He stood motionless, utterly confused about what action to take next. Around him, the uplifting clarity of the sky was dissolving into frightening darkness, taking with it the colorful garden that had welcomed them a couple of minutes ago. The background had suddenly turned to a nightmarish penumbra, distorting everything surrounding him, while her abject words, as sharp as blood-thirsty blades, slashed through his soul.

"You don't have to answer, Adil. Your eyes speak for you… your whole body does."

She sighed, looked away then spoke again, "You're a nice guy. I owe you the truth. In fact, I owe it to myself."

Adil wished she would stop talking, but she didn't, "If you think that I have never been with a man, you are wrong."

Although his eyes were opened, he couldn't see her anymore. Her voice, however, was unfortunately still reaching him.

"I am not that pure, innocent girl you want and choose to see me as. I am not the woman who awaits you to teach her what pleasure is. Nor am I the wife whom you desire to own and shape so that she may love you, and only you, hour after hour, day and night, throughout the years, until her life, that life she fully dedicated to serving you, finally expires. No, Adil. I am not that woman who doesn't mind sacrificing herself so that you can feel like a real man."

Adil wanted to cry, but a man doesn't cry, or so did his father claim. He knew that he would feel better if he did, but he would never disobey his father. Never. How he wished he could be like his father, less of a coward, then he would show her, then he would teach her. But he had no strength, no will to reclaim his trampled pride.

"Adil, I don't even think I am capable of falling in love. Do you understand me?"

He felt her hand touch his forearm, as if reaching for an answer. He would never forget how he speechlessly acceded. Nor would he forget nodding acquiescently to that other question she then asked if he still wanted to marry her.

"Then pick a date," she spoke coldly while looking at

his somberly ashen face, "and tell your parents that I have accepted. I'll tell mine."

Lowering her eyes, she spun around and started walking away. Her blurry silhouette faded in the growing distance separating his body from hers.

As frozen as Adil was, he could still feel the needling of every word she had dropped at her wake; words that drifted behind her, all the way to his ears, "I don't love you. I might never love you… but I promise you that I'll try."

Inside him, tears pressed and pressed seeking a way out. But the doctor stood his ground. The woman he had fallen in love with had just humiliated him beyond repair. She had torn his world into shreds, in no more than a few minutes. There was nowhere for him hide.

Not knowing what to do, say, or think, the future groom remained still, as if paralyzed, unaware of time, until something within, like a tiny unexpected spark that is ignited in complete darkness, a spark that refuses to die and instead continues to grow brighter and brighter until it burns all of the surrounding darkness.

Slowly, Adil began accepting his fate. He accepted his lot, and once he did so, fate didn't seem that bad after all. Then, and despite the harshness of the words that had been uttered, he somehow started believing that there was a silver lining to the deal made. "Yes," he thought, standing between weak conviction and strong denial, "She is a beautiful woman, and I want her. She will be mine, since that is her wish, and I will teach her to love me. I will teach her to care about me, and then everything will be fine, and everything she said today will be forgotten."

Adil chose to believe that all would go according to

his plans, even when in actuality he hadn't done much planning. Thus, lost in a self-erected fantasy, he failed to see the importance of the choice he was making. He failed to see how far-reaching the consequences of his stance would be, not only for him, but for his mother, for as soon as the good news reached Fatma, who, by then, as if caught too deep in the bourgeois character she had been playing out of motherly love, decided that by having united her son, her flesh and blood, to such a respectable and prestigious family, she had become a better person, gaining status and rising up the social ladder of who's-who at once, from a mere Bedouin housewife to a truly sophisticated lady.

From then on, Fatma began behaving differently, thinking herself a born Fassi, and consequentially making herself the laughing stock of those whom she used to consider friends, as well as of real Fassi women whom she tried her hardest to resemble, choosing to be blind to the fact that these women of a different social milieu not only could never accept her as one of their own, but in fact, saw her as a pathetic embarrassment to her own family, a fake, a phony, a 'nouveau-riche,' a pathetic poser.

After a while, even her husband grew tired of her, for in his eyes, she was no longer the caring wife he had shared life with. She was no longer the woman he had loved. She had become a stranger, someone he could neither respect nor love, for as he firmly believed, 'You are the company you keep,' and the company she kept was one he had warned her against, again and again, for as the proverb goes, 'Wear the shoes that fit you.' That, he believed, was in summary the way to happiness, not running after names and prestige and whatever it was she was chasing after.

For some time, he warned her, again and again, about those people whom he stayed away from even during his son's wedding, which he had attended but not enjoyed, "And how could I enjoy the company of such arrogant folks," he had complained, "especially that pompous Minister who seems to think himself God himself –May God, the Compassionate, forgive the comparison I am making, for no one is comparable to the Almighty, although that fat fool doesn't seem to know that. May the wrath of the All-Sustaining fall on him and his kind. They are all crooked, I tell you. They fatten themselves on the back of this poor country's citizens. They're selling our country and its resources, bit by bit, to foreigners who don't give a damn about us, and call their ruinous schemes economical savvy."

Thus he went, his views growing in acerbity with each passing day, "And did you just see his house? Did you? How do you think a Minister gets to own so much, when most people can barely afford a single decent meal a day? How does a Minister become so blind to the plight of those he is supposed to care for and so consumed by his own desires? May God cut off his thieving hands and pluck out his greedy eyes. May God Almighty protect us against his wiles. May He rid us of all politicians wherever they may be. They're all thieves! Yes thieves of the worst breed, and what else would you call those who starve the newborn and even the one who is yet to be born, to feed their bottomless greed."

Fatma tried her best to change his man, but the man was, as she herself put it, more stubborn than toothless mule, so after a while she tired and gave up on sweetening his views. He stood his ground, and she hers. He was unwavering, as he'd always been. She had changed, and could no longer reconnect with, what she now conceived as, his backward ways. Realizing that he had lost his touch, probably to old age, Adil's father just let the wife he now saw as irremediably lost do as she pleased, hoping that one blessed day, God willing, she might regain the priceless ability to recognize what is right from what isn't. However and until that day arrived, he did what any grudge-imbibed early septuagenarian, with as much money as he had, more than enough to support his family, perhaps for the next three generations, would do. He went ahead and found himself a second wife, a younger woman, as it is the norm, a woman the age of one of his grand-daughters, with the hope that her youth and energy would make him forget his worries, brighten his nights, and rekindle his passion for life. "And, why not," he argued, "when God, the All-Giving, allows it?" adding to heartbroken Fatma and to his protesting children, "Who are you to judge me? I have worked hard to give you everything you have, thanks to God. Don't I deserve a little happiness?"

"But, Haj, she is twenty-two, and you…" before they could finish the glowering groom-to-be threw his hands in the air, shaken with anger, and cried, 'Jealous! You're all jealous of me. All of you. May God, the All-Knowing, be my witness. May he support me against your wicked schemes. Crows! You dream of feasting on my dead body. You're just waiting for me to die so you can inherit my money… Well, well, let me tell you something…"

So, they begged him to calm down, think about his

health, and forgive them because, after all, all they really wanted was his happiness, no more, no less, adding, to prove their love and affection, "If a second wife is what you desire, then, who are we to argue," after which, silence fell, a sign for them to get up, kiss his head, and depart, which was exactly what they did, one by one, leaving Fatma, alone and lost to her new fate.

Blind to the Fates' whimsical doings, Adil stood by and chose to believe in dreams, unable to guess that by acquiescing the very way he had done, he was affecting that which mattered the most to him -his father's feelings toward him. Little did he realize that the man who had always shown pride in his highly educated son would soon distance himself from a character whose weaknesses he hadn't perceived until Yasmine stepped into their lives, revealing what the son he had raised, and in whom he had invested so much, was truly like.

It was as if the scales had fallen of the Haj's eyes, so that suddenly, his highest source of joy was nothing more than a spineless individual with a medical degree. "And how can I respect someone who doesn't respect himself? How can I feel closeness to someone who looks down on his own people? A Berber is a Berber," insisted the patriarch, "That is what I am, what my father was, what his father was before him, and I could go back like this until the very source of our bloodline. Berbers! That is what we are. May God be my sustaining witness."

There were even instances when alone, or thinking himself alone, many, in his office, and at home, heard him mutter, "Idiot," or "Fool," or "Blind," or even, "No son of mine," and although startled for a second by the blurted insult, they would quickly figure who was in his mind. Undoubtedly, he loved his son. But how could he express his love for someone who pained him so much? How could he show his affection toward those who reject their very nature, and thus a whole world, a Berber world, his world, with all the affinities of its spoken language, the flavors of its foods, the colors of its dresses, the uniqueness of its culture, and the richness of its history? No, he couldn't forgive, no matter his feelings. The deed was done. His son was no longer his, but even this loss was made bearable once his second wife announced she was pregnant, which the old father took as a blessing from He who in his infinite wisdom gives it all and takes it all back, a claimant gesture meant to alleviate the deep sorrow that had been born from Adil's disappointments.

Yasmine Berrada and Adil Khadir, married now for six years and some days, sit facing one another, separated by their square oak kitchen table. They're in the same room, at the same table, seemingly having breakfast together. Yet, for being unable, and somehow unwilling, to connect, they both feel alone, divided by a soporifically enveloping and protectively thick silence. Both the breakfast and the silence are part of a routine that is deeply embedded in their lonely lives, a dull ritual to which they have both become accustomed.

Adil is stirring a teaspoon in his favorite coffee mug, while skimming rather absent-mindedly through today's newspaper. In front of him, almost at arms reach, Yasmine takes a bite of a toasted piece of bread lightly moistened with butter, while focusing on the texture of the toast she is holding with her right hand between thumb and middle finger. Between the two of them, there isn't much left to say.

Truthfully, they may as well not even be together. But then again, there are the parents with their precious feelings and high expectations, even when the same parents are, in fact have been, and that even before the wedding day, well aware of the unhappiness that was born out of their matrimonial union.

Isolated in the silence of yet another morning, they each begin daydreaming. Their minds drift away, escaping the binding and often unbreakable rules of reality, leading them to ponder about different options, possibilities and lived lives. But, as it is usually the case, for this is not the first time, they catch themselves partaking in this helpless state of wishful thinking, and immediately dismiss these thoughts that are too complicated to be given any real consideration.

They raise their objections, the same ones that were used yesterday and the day before that. Their argument is the same, day after day, a very simple and fatalistic one. "This is my life. This is what was fated for me. Life is a test. And, how could I be so selfish anyway? There is so much to consider, so much to go against. How would I answer the inescapable, 'What would people think and say?' And let us not forget the overly used, 'Don't be hasty, just wait and everything will work itself out.' No, there is no way out of this one; all I can do is pretend. The world is watching as if everyone else's happiness depends directly on the show we have been, are and will be performing.'"

As far as they're both concerned, no one cares about their feelings. As far as they both believe, no one wants to know about their needs. That is why they're sitting, suffocating in silence, abnegating their innermost yearnings, coping anyway, and everyway, they can, Yasmine juggling more work than anyone should handle, Adil seeking the understanding smile and the comforting voice of Najat Hawaz, his assistant, the woman he secretly loves with every fiber of his being, the woman he desperately longs for.

Life goes on. No one realizes that Yasmine is burying herself under mountains of work to escape a sense of cowardice that keeps her from acting. No one guesses that soft spoken Najat is Adil's reason for rushing through traffic on his way to work, as well as for hating Sundays and every gruesome holiday that deprives him of the woman his heart is beating for. Life goes on. Everything appearing as it should be. Meanwhile, whenever Adil lies in bed, he dreams of his assistant. Eyes closed, his back turned to his wife, he shamelessly fantasizes about the one his heart truly yearns for.

Every night, in complete darkness, fully awake, Adil dreams of closeness, of intimacy with the only woman he really cares about. He dreams of Najat Hawaz and wonders where she is and whom she is with when not at work. He wishes he could confess the nature of his feelings towards her, although he suspects that Najat could read his mind because of the way she sometimes has to stand at his opened office door, just staring at him, her eyes brimming, as if with sadness, her face flushed, as if with hope —perhaps the same hope that keeps him going.

Hope. Adil lives on hope. He hopes for impossible change. He hopes for forbidden happiness. He hopes to find enough strength to take charge of his own destiny. He hopes that when the day arrives, when he'll finally be brave enough and strong enough to stand up for what he really desires, for her, she will still be there waiting for him and not gone away, having grown too tired and too desperate, because he has taken too long.

Aroused by his muse's name, fragrance and beauty, Adil's body resists the call of sleep. He turns and churns, oblivious to Yasmine's physical closeness, not interested the least in knowing if she is aware of his restlessness, or even if she can guess whom it is he is thinking of. He goes on wishing for Najat to be his. He prays for a miracle, for divine intervention, for salvation.

Adil prays unaware that, in such moments, in a house on the other side of town, a golden haired woman, with aquatic green eyes, tired of lying to her mother about her reasons for refusing each and every bachelor that has come

knocking at their door with the clear intention of propos-
ing, stares longingly at the ceiling, praying for the doctor
to reach out and for the wife to let go. "Why not," she
would add, "He doesn't love her anyway, and moreover
she -that cold demon he was tricked into marrying- can't
give him what he wants."

"Poor Doctor Khadir. To learn, the way he did, seven
months after his wedding, and after the dozen medical
tests performed on both of them, that it is she who is infertile, so infertile that not even the most famous charlatans,
conventional medicine having failed, could make a grain
of difference in her case. Meanwhile here I am, denied of
love, frustrated to the point that sleep eludes me, wishing
I could be more than my soul-mate's confident, ready to
give him what he desires and undeniably deserves."

Najat prays for the witch to break her spell, go away,
disappear out of is life. She prays, and prays, for Yasmine
Berrada to let go of the man who has never been hers to
hold. With tears in her eyes, she curses the woman whom
she blames for her sorrow, unaware that in the Doctor's
domicile, at that exact moment, Yasmine is wishing for
the living nightmare to end, for Adil to act honestly and
stop pretending. If only he would agree to the divorce offer she has made him a hundred times over. If only he'd
stop being so afraid of disappointing his family. His father
had passed away, yet he was still doing his best to please
the Haj. "I'll ask him again tomorrow," decides Yasmine,
"What else is there to do in a country where a woman
isn't entitled to petition for divorce?" she closes her eyes,
"Tomorrow. Tomorrow. Another day. Another chance."

Najat sighs and closes her eyes, breathing out her
frustration toward a wife she thinks she can read as an

opened recipe book, a selfish heartbreaker. Never in her mind, could she believe how Yasmine feels about that marriage of hers. But then again, how could Najat intuit the truth? How could she know that Yasmine, despite a lack of faith in God and in anything that isn't founded on hard evidence and unshakable logic, is praying for this tragic farce to come to an end, prays for peace.

Six years of marriage and a few more days, Adil gets up from the table and, without a word, turns around and heads out. Yasmine simply sits there staring at her toast. He closes the apartment door behind him and walks to the elevator. He is tired of the way his life is going, yet he is incapable of effecting any change to his situation. His father's dead, yet he cannot handle his disapproval, even from the grave. He wishes things were different. He wishes for flowers and laughter, children and their noise, homemade meals cooked with care and love… But, ever since the beginning, she had made it so hard… and God knows how hard he had tried, even against his own judgment and heart. The elevator's door opens up. He steps into the steel box, takes a deep breath and presses the ground-floor button.

Alone in the kitchen, with no sound to distract her from a pressing silence that seems to imbue everything in the apartment with guilt, Yasmine wonders why she persists on going on, when life is hard, and so painful. She asks, "Why not die and put an end to all this nonsense? Why hurt and be hurt? Why?" She looks around her, searching for answers, or maybe, for the courage to end a life she cannot live any longer. She closes her eyes, wishing she weren't such a coward. Then and with a sigh, she prays for forgiveness from a man who once tried his hardest, and curses the one who once ruined her heart.

"Who are they?" asked five year old Youssef, pointing to a man and a young boy standing against a crackled wall in an old black and white picture that hung in a wooden frame on the living room wall, to the left of the kitchen door.

Isaam put down the newspaper he had been reading, smiled at his son and replied, "The boy is your grandfather; my father."

"Your father?"

"Yes, that's my father," nodded Isaam.

Perplexed by the answer Youssef stared at the boy wearing the traditional robe Moroccan men often wear –especially those from the countryside and older ones in the cities; a sturdy djelabah that looked a few sizes larger than it should have been, and then said, "but, Bassidoo is old."

Isaam let out a soft chuckle and explained, "He is old now, but in this picture he was a young boy, only a few years older than you are... I think that that picture was taken a very long time ago. I would say, more than sixty years ago."

Youssef looked at the boy and tried to recognize the grandfather who lived in the riff valley, at the base of a mountain, in a large farm house, where his father had been periodically taking the whole family once every year, and where he had spent a few weeks, no longer than three months ago, running after chickens and petting fluffy bunnies, "Mmh..."

"Can't you see that it's your grandfather?"

Youssef shook his head, squinting at the picture. Unable to find any resemblance between the child in the black and white photo, and the old man he called Bassidoo, one being too young and the other too old, Youssef gave up and turned his attention to the strangely accoutered scurvy fellow wrapped in a combination of black and white fabrics loosely hanging over his proudly standing frame, and whose penetrating gaze shooting from underneath a wrapped white turban seemed too piercing to be ignored.

Isaam, guessing the change in his son's subject of interest, explained, "The man standing next to your Bassidoo is his father. He is your great grandfather and his name is Ahmed Jazil."

The boy raised his head and stared at his father, "I never met him."

Isaam glanced at the picture and then back at his son, "He disappeared a long time ago, many years before you were born."

Youssef walked to his father and sat next to him, "...like grandma?" He spoke, vividly remembering walking in the funeral procession that had followed the wrapped and lifeless body of his grandmother, a woman he had only met once, but of whom he kept the sweetest memory, so much had she spoiled him with handfuls of candy and platefuls of delicious pastries.

Isaam put his right hand on his son's head and replied, "Sort of..."

Youssef gave his father a curious look. His father sighed. The boy was waiting for more details, but none seemed to be coming. He glanced at the man in the picture, and noticing that a riffle was slung over his shoulder asked, "Why does he have a gun?"

"He was a feedaee."

"A feedaee?" asked Youssef, tilting his head the way

he usually did when unable to understand the meaning of some word.

"A feedaee is someone who fought to liberate our country," Isaam grinned, realizing that the conversation was going to be a long one. He adjusted himself over the sofa to lean against the pillow that was waiting behind him, and began explaining, "You see, many years ago, before I was born, the Frenchmen came to our country. They came with riffles and canons, and started controlling our people. They began telling our parents what to do and how to think. They started taking away our treasures without giving us anything in exchange. They made us work for them and didn't pay us much. And when we complained, do you know what they did?"

"What?" asked the boy.

Isaam took a deep breath and narrowed his eyes, taking a moment to allow his mind to sift through those memories from harsher times –times, he was glad, his son didn't know much about, "The foreigners beat and hurt our people. Sometimes, when they got really angry for not getting what they wanted, or just to teach our people a lesson, they even used their guns to kill them. So, of course, our people didn't like that at all, and why should they? Weren't they after all in their own country? Do you understand?"

The boy nodded.

Isaam brushed his moustache three times with index and thumb, looking pensive, and then picked up the thread of his story where he'd dropped it, "The brave people of this land of ours didn't need anyone to come and tell them what to do. They surely didn't need anyone to come and steal our treasures, to make them, and their children after them, and by children I mean us, work for barely anything. No, our people didn't need these greedy foreigners to take over our lands and lives, to enslave us so that we may do their biding and punish us if we refused to obey."

Isaam closed his eyes for a second and sighed, "But the foreigners came anyway. And before we could do anything about it, the Spaniards arrived and treated us as if we were less valuable than dogs, and maybe a little worst. I guess, they really believed that because they had a lot of guns they could call us savages and take advantage of us. What they didn't realize was that our people were brave, that they had courage in their hearts and God by their side.

So that soon men and women, heroes, like your great grandfather stood up, ready to fight those who wanted to control our land and people. They armed themselves with whatever weapons they could get their hands on and faced the enemy's army. They faced a large force, better armed and better trained. They resisted. They faced evil men, and fought harder than the soldiers who were terrorizing and hurting our families. They fought because there was no other choice. They hid in the cities, the mountains, the desert and the countryside. They attacked their enemies everywhere, whenever, and as often as they could, until the Frenchmen and the Spaniards couldn't stand it anymore, until they finally decided that it was better for them to leave."

Isaam rubbed his son's back, and watched him grimace while trying to make sense of what he had just heard. He grinned and continued, "Your great grandfather was a brave warrior, who fought in the trenches and the northern mountains, and never surrendered. Then, after him your grandfather, followed in his father's footsteps. He became a feedaee, a man ready to die for his people's freedom, who, along others who had fought and risked their lives, was able to bring us freedom and allow us to declare our independence as a country. You see, it is thanks to these heroes that we can live the way we are living. It is thanks to them that we live in dignity. Do you understand?"

Youssef nodded again, but with little conviction. Then, he looked back at the picture and asked, "What happened to Basidoo's father?"

"No one knows for sure." replied Isaam, eyes on the picture, "My father told me about a battalion of Spaniards led by an officer named Franco. Franco's battalion had attacked his village, while most of the men from the village were gone fighting somewhere in the mountains. When your grandfather and his comrades returned, their homes were all burnt down. There were no survivors to be found. Your great grandfather, looked for your great grandmother and his three daughters and two sons, but couldn't find them. Devastated, he cried and raised his arms to the skies and swore that he would make those who were responsible pay for their hideous crimes. He picked his gun and left the village in pursuit of the Spanish officer named Franco, accompanied by a few others."

Youssef's eyes were wide open, as he loved action stories, and this one was proving to be a great one, given that it involved someone to whom he was actually related.

"Your great grandfather and his companions were never seen again. Although some say that they actually caught up with and fought Franco's men at least a dozen times. Unfortunately, Franco was a cunning officer and a formidable opponent. He was very hard to beat. In his own country, people saw him as a great hero. In fact, they revered him so much that when he returned to Spain, he became that country's ruler."

"And great-Bassidoo?"

"He disappeared after Franco was called back to Spain. My father once told that great-Bassidoo followed his enemy, Franco, there." Isaam shook his head, "The sad thing is that he never found out that his wife and children were still alive. He never found out that they had miraculously escaped the massacre by running away. They ran away and took refuge in a nearby forest, which they knew very well, as soon as the first shots were heard. They hid for days, without knowing if they could go back or not. When they returned, it was too late. Your great grandfather had already left... and they would never see him again."

Sitting in her office, surrounded by walls of books and folders; walls that she has come to see as the very borders of her sanctuary, Yasmine turns page after page, her hazel eyes squinting behind corrective lenses held in by a thin and almost invisible wire frame, attentively looking for answers in a massively intimidating, leather-bound law book that lay open, in front of her, on the center of large mahogany desk. On her occupational throne, a fading maroon leather chair, she is so focused and lost in her work that it shows on the face she never embellishes with make-up.

The telephone, set on the right side of her desk, beeps. She frowns, gives it an impatient look, and presses the speaker-phone button that automatically connects her to her secretary. "Yes Aicha, what is it?"

"Excuse me, Madame. Your mother is holding on line three. She says it is important that you take her call."

Yasmine shakes her head and says, "Thank you Aicha, I'll take it."

"You are very welcome Madame," responds the understandingly sounding voice in the box.

Yasmine sighs, removes her glasses, sets them in front of her on the desk, and then reservedly presses the number three button.

"Yes, mother, what's going on?"

"Dear, dear, dear… How times have changed," starts the soft and very sophisticated voice on the other side of the line, "I remember days when people used to begin their conversations by saying hello and how are you."

"Mother, please I am defending a client in a few hours. So, I hope that you'll forgive me for not adhering to the rules of telephone etiquette and for not having time for small talk right now. Is there anything I can do for you?"

Unperturbed and in control, the voice responds, "Darling, there is no need for you to explain yourself. Don't you worry about your mother's feelings."

Yasmine tenses around the neck and shoulders, thinking "Here comes the guilt."

"The reason I am calling is to ask you to meet someone I have invited for dinner tonight."

"What for?" asks Yasmine before adding, "I am already married."

"Just trust me, will you?" says Lalla Amina very calmly, her voice conveying the unshakable confidence she has always been well-known for, "It is for your own good."

"For my own… good. Yes." Yasmine resists a sudden urge to say what she really feels. She presses her lips into a tight line, reluctantly muffling honesty, even when honesty, she imagines, would feel so satisfyingly appropriate right now. Yes, how she wishes she could just throw open the floodgates, releasing all that pent-up frustration she's been reluctantly harboring within.

However being the somewhat dignified daughter she has been thus far has its drawbacks. There are standards to be maintained and expectations to be met. She looks around. She looks at the walls and then at the plainness of her office's ceiling, searching for a way out, a means of escape before saying something she might dearly regret later. A black and white scene from some Houdini documentary arises and dissolves.

"You will not regret it, I promise."

Yasmine straightens her back, takes a deep breath, before clearing her throat the way she would have done had she been addressing a judge or a large crowd, and asks, "What are you talking about? Is this another one of your charlatans, or as you prefer referring to them, mystics? Because, Mother, and I don't mean to be disrespectful by saying this, if it is, then, I would rather be excused."

"Yasmine, I know how you don't believe in these things, and I understand your point of view, but please, I would really appreciate it if you showed up tonight… Please, do it for me, as a favor, How about that?"

Yasmine remembers that this woman who is now pleading over the phone, no matter how frustrating, is nonetheless her mother, and this makes her feel guilty for having spoken so harshly and disrespectfully, so much that for a second she considers acquiescing. But, being the attorney she is, she continues arguing instead, "Mother, can't you see that it's a waste of time and money? I mean…"

"Yasmine, please, I am asking you to do me a favor tonight. Please, don't say no. Just come over. I promise you that it's different this time."

Guilt strikes again, as if to separate the loving daughter from the no-nonsense lawyer, pleading to one and silencing the other. Yasmine wavers as two of the most irreconcilable and conflicting aspects of her personality clash in a struggle of will. The overachieving professional in her takes the blow, resists one more time, and goes on probing, "How different could it be?"

The mother sighs and says, "Well, for starters, he is not from here. Then, finding him was very hard and convincing him to meet you tonight, even harder. And finally, the man is only passing by. He plans on leaving the city tomorrow. But all this is beside the point. Please,

I am begging you, just come for a nice meal tonight, will you?"

"Mother, when will you learn?" Yasmine wishes she could be in control. She is sick of being manipulated, especially since she is in her office, in her element. "I am so tired of these plans of yours. Tell me, how many times did you believe and say that it would work? And how many times did it actually work?" The debater within regains her confidence. Behind these walls, she is the decision-maker. "I am sorry, but I am too busy this week." Today, she will stand her ground, weather the storm, and, when the deed is done, enjoy her victory. "I will have to decline your invitation."

That is when the tone of Lalla Amina's voice, which while remaining audibly the same, hardens as the undeniably strong will of one brought up amidst nobility and prestige surfaces, "Yasmine, don't forget that I am your mother. Never doubt that I will keep on doing all that is in my power, and even more, to help you. All I want is your happiness. Surely you understand that I will not stand by and watch my only daughter give up on her share of joy in this life. You can hate me if you want. You can think me a fool for believing what I believe. You can think whatever you want to think of me. None of this will alter the fact that I am your mother. I love you and care for you. And that is why I will bring him to you wherever you are, if you do not show up tonight."

Yasmine stifles a heartfelt protest, realizing that any effort toward changing her mother's mind would be a waste of time. So instead she chooses to remain silent.

"Yasmine, come on… Yasmine?"

Defeated, the daughter asks, "What time?"

"Eight. Okay."

"Sure."

"Yasmine?"

"Yes?"

"I promise you won't regret it."

Yasmine sighs, "I'll see you at eight then."

For a minute, she stares blankly at the door, promising herself that one day she will stop complying with her mother's absurd wishes. The distant sound of a door slamming pulls her out of her meditations. She slowly turns her attention to her desk, begins gathering the file folders and contract forms she will need today, setting everything in an order reflective of her schedule, in a black leather-bound briefcase. She checks the briefcase's content one more time, before locking it. Then she stands, grabs her gray vest, whose color matches the pants she is wearing, and, sets it over her forearm.

Checking her reflection in the mirror, she looks for any visual flaw that might lessen the visual impact she has learned to create, through both attire and demeanor, in her role of implacable attorney. Quickly, she readjusts the collar of her short sleeve white button-down shirt, leaving its top button open. In the mirror, she sees an unwavering figure, sharp and smooth, unforgiving the way the unsheathed blade of a warrior aught to be, and is satisfied.

When she comes out of her office and closes the door behind her, she's already forgotten about the upsetting telephone conversation, her mother, and the dinner invitation. Her eyes gleam with determination as she walks out of the office building. With light, quick, and precise steps, she assertively cuts through the crowded sidewalks, completely oblivious to all the admiring eyes glued on that radiant beauty of hers -a characteristic she construes as a hindrance, a superficial trait she does her best to muffle and veil, but somehow miserably fails to subdue in any meaningful way.

Yasmine is undeniably attractive despite the unflattering glasses and the tamed hair she tightly pulls back and gathers at the base of her skull; sensual despite the simple white shirt, the conservative gray pants, the matching vest she holds over her left arm and the black briefcase she carries in her right hand; and irresistible despite the absence of lipstick and eyeliner on a face she keeps as colorless as a blank canvas.

Yes, Yasmine is a stunningly beautiful appearance, perhaps as much as ten years ago, when she crossed this same street, moving more like a graceful ballerina, the balls of her feet barely touching the ground, as light as a cotton cloud peacefully traveling above the city's skyline, smiling at life and all its wonders, effortlessly reflecting the brightness of a warm sun and the vastness of a clear blue sky, her long wavy hair freely mingling with the breeze, her white summer dress flowing freely as if caught in a current of grace, and her eyes -pearls of hazel- glistening with passion, with hunger for the sight of her sweet beloved.

In those days, love could be seen radiating through her every feature, as she moved across streets, avenues and boulevards, carried by the fragrance of her lover... A young man, hardly six months older than herself, whom she had noticed two years earlier on a hot summer day, while sun-bathing in the company of five girlfriends from high school, on the soft sands of what was her favorite beach.

It was mid-morning. He was running, wearing nothing more than a blue pair of swim trunks, chasing after a ball, pursued by a dozen other guys. He was light and quick. Fully in control of his athletic legs, he tackled, kicked, dribbled and finally scored with amazing skill. She couldn't take her eyes off of him. She was almost entranced by his presence, more so since he too had noticed her. She could tell that he had, because every now and then, while still trotting or sprinting, in one direction or the other, he would look at her and smile, eyes aglow with such intensity they caused Yasmine to almost blush and look away.

But Yasmine refused to turn her gaze away. And why should she? She had never been shy. She had never been intimidated by boys. She knew better. She was the daughter of a powerful and charismatic man. Yet, there was no denying that she was getting rather tingly and warm inside. She remembered that she wasn't alone. She wondered if he could tell, or worst, if the girls could tell. She hated appearing weak, the way woman were portrayed in certain romance novels and Egyptian TV series.

Assuming an air of nonchalance, she turned and reached into her backpack, as if she were looking for something. When she was done, a slight smile of satisfaction curled her lips to the left. None of her classmates had been paying attention to her, as they were, along with an interested crowd, following the game, which was actually very entertaining, especially with tension growing between the two teams, given that money, as is usually the case in such events, was hanging in the balance. As it was, and although her favorite player had scored two goals, his team was down by three points. Their opponents, bigger, older and much more aggressive, had managed to put five goals in, and were determined to keep the results in their favor.

At half-time, and to her surprise, the young man sprinted toward her and stopped in front of her beach towel. He was tan with untidy brown hair turned reddish by the sun. In his confident brown eyes was a softness that contrasted with the rest of his lean-yet-well-defined body.

"Hi," he squatted down stretching his right arm with an open palm.

Yasmine propped herself up, on her forearms and elbows, and looked him coolly in the eyes, while the other girls, startled by his intrusion, frowned at him distrustfully.

He kept his attention on her, ignoring the others, "I'm Youssef. What is your name?"

The other girls' gaze shot her way, as she replied, voice ringing with confidence, "Sorry. I don't give my name to strangers."

Her voice clear and unwavering, like a sweet melody, echoed in his heart. He nodded, maintaining eye contact, "Technically, I am not a stranger. I just told you my name, Youssef."

The other girls started giggling and teasing him with biting comments meant to shatter the bravest of fools' ambitions. But Youssef didn't move, or even raise an eyebrow. He may as well have been made of stone. Somehow, their reaction had barely registered in his ears before being swept by the wind into the ocean's immensity stretching behind him. He was staring at her, watching her take her time, shamelessly examining him from head to toe, test-

ing his nerves, and didn't seem to mind that his hand was
still hanging in the air.

"Yasmine," she offered, almost neutrally.

Youssef repeated her name inside his head, so as to
never forget it.

"So," she asked, "What do you want, Youssef?"

"I have a proposition for you, Yasmine," he grinned
assertively, eyes full of what seemed to be sweet malice.

Yasmine's nodded, completely oblivious to one of her
friends' dismissing, as well as disbelieving, laughter. "A
proposition," she repeated, "What kind of proposition?"

He recognized a hint of interest surfacing in her voice
—in fact, it was so obvious that everyone around her could
tell, "It's very simple. I've noticed that you've been following the game for a while now, and I am sure that you
know my team is losing." he paused, allowing his eyes to
softly meet hers.

"And?" she tried to sound uninterested, but her expression and voice easily betrayed the excitement that was
spreading within, like a wave, rising and moving, aching
to burst.

"Well, here's the deal, if my team wins I would like
you to honor me with your company for a celebratory
drink at that café over there, behind you," he paused as
if to watch her reaction, then added after widening his
smile, creating two symmetrically positioned dimples on
the inner sides of his cheeks, slightly above the edges of
his lips, "Just you and I."

"You're crazy!" she exclaimed shaking her head.

His dimples shyly disappeared, yet the pleasant smile
lingered, unabashed by the outbursts of taunting laughter

his offer had engendered. Then, unwaveringly he inquired, "What do you say? Do we have a deal?"

Yasmine sat up, leaning forward, followed by five pairs of wide opened and very expecting eyes which had become inescapably absorbed by the exchange. "I'll accept it, if you agree to a condition I have."

He leaned a little closer, "Which is?"

Eyes widened. Bodies tensed and froze. The girls couldn't wait to hear what Yasmine had in mind.

"My condition is that you score all the remaining goals." feeling in control, she smiled defiantly.

The dimples returned before he responded with a voice as calm and cool as that morning's shore, "You got it."

She reached out with her right hand, finally grabbed his and shook it firmly.

Youssef sprang up, threw her a wink and said, "Be ready," before running back to his teammates, who, as soon as he joined them, started teasing him about where he was and what he might have been saying.

When the second half of the game started, all six girls were already sitting upright on their beach towels, waiting to see Youssef in action. They followed his every move with eyes hardly blinking, faces flush with expectations. There was no denying he was a talented footballer. Within five minutes of the whistle blow, he had managed to score two more goals, and was sauntering across the sandy field as if the deal was in the pocket, flashing a grand smile in Yasmine's direction. Even the girls were beginning to believe that he could win the bet.

The five girls relaxed and turned their attention to Yasmine who, unable to remove her eyes from the game, did her best at ignoring the teasing remarks that were beginning to rain on her. Suddenly, Yasmine cringed, raising one hand in front of her mouth. The game had stopped. Youssef was lying on the sand, curled into a ball. His face was contorted with pain, as he held on to his ankle with both hands.

"What happened?" asked one of the classmates.

Yasmine lowered her hand. She tried to speak, but just couldn't. Youssef had been kicked so brutally that it had to have been with the obvious ill-intention of taking him out, and even if that meant seriously hurting him. The move had been performed with such viciousness Yasmine was certain Youssef's ankle was broken. She stood up, worried about him, and feeling guilty for having incited him to win.

But Youssef was still in. He would not be taken down, not that day. Instead he simply and forcefully hit the sand with his right palm before jumping back on his feet, ready for more action. Standing tall and challenging, he grabbed the ball, dropped it down and sat his right foot on it. He scanned the field and all its players, then focused his burning gaze on the one who had hit him and who, surrounded by some his own teammates, offered not an apology but instead a vicious smirk and a menacing look.

Youssef's bare chest rose and expanded slowly. His eyes narrowed, fixated on his aggressor, Kadour -the bull, as he was known, within the streets of his neighborhood and in the many makeshift fields of Casablanca's five districts, for an abnormally massive forehead and wide neck, as well as for his overtly aggressive behavior and short temperament. The bull, short but built like a thick wall, was known for many things. A bully in the fields, he was proud of his reputation and never missed a chance to show how ruthless he could be. The scars that marked his tough face were those of an ex-con with a long criminal record, a conniving thief, a pimp whenever the occasion arose, a smoker of hash and a heavy drinker.

Kadour clenched his fists and grinned. He was waiting for the fight to begin. For a while now, he'd been relishing the opportunity to humiliate Youssef, and of course, mangle his annoying and pretty face. Yasmine's chest tightened. Blood rushed into her stomach releasing both fear and panic. She felt weak in the silence that hovered over everyone present. Youssef glanced at Yasmine. His features softened, and he managed a smile. Then suddenly, and without any warning, he made a short pass and sprinted forward, bringing the game back on. The bull, rubbed of his moment, spat at the sand, and reluctantly turned around to follow a bouncing ball he was no longer interested in.

Too far already, Youssef was moving beyond pain, feeling utterly unbreakable, unstoppable. And within a few seconds, he adroitly dribbled his way through five players, reminding some of the legendary Pele, and scored a third goal, bringing both teams to a tie.

The girls, along with a growing circle of spectators who having recognized a good game had been gathering in throngs, cheered him on, the way they would have for a football star. Inspired by all the recognition he was now getting, Youssef started playing with more skill and determination than he had ever thought himself possessing, so that even Kadour, tired from running after him, decided to stop bothering and just stand by the goalkeeper.

A few minutes to end of the battle, Youssef scored another goal, bringing victory to his team. For the opponents, that goal was the final straw that broke their bruised morale and unity, they began arguing and shouting at one another, even when, according to a nervous referee in charge of handing out the winners cash prize, the game had ended.

Without a second's delay, overtaken with excitement, and keeping to her word, Yasmine started putting on a pair of green denim shorts and a white fitted tank-top over her two-piece bathing suit. Suddenly and just as she was about to put on her green flip-flops, a loud commotion resonated and made her look up. A fight had started between some of the opposing players. They had clashed, forming a single moving entity, within which confines blows were being exchanged, even as the rest of the players, charged with adrenaline, were frantically running around the perimeter of the melee trying to find a way in, ready to participate, eager to give and receive. She tried to locate Youssef within the moving crowd, but could not discern him. She tried to get closer, but her friends would not let her go. They surrounded her, holding her arms, begging her to stay put and calm down.

Yasmine thought of Kadour, his frightening face, his brutish body. The thought of him made her feel weak in the legs. She stood there, heart pounding, unable to do anything but let worry gnaw at her insides, as she watched and waited, along with the other girls and all the amused spectators who, always happy to be entertained gratuitously, were still surrounding, from a safe distance, the colliding footballers.

Suddenly, and as quickly as it had started, the fight broke up and the crowd started dispersing in every possible direction, as if nothing had happened, as if the losing team had not complained, had not called the winners cheaters who had bribed the obviously biased, son of a swine, referee, and of course, had not then, categorically refused to let go of their money. No, it was as if none of that happened. There was simply no proof of violence in this almost deserted stretch of beach, on which there was no one else but a group of seven young people, standing in front of some towels and bags, pretending not to notice two police officers, walking in easily recognizable –even from a great distance- gray uniforms.

The uniformed men were probably on one of their daily excruciatingly hot patrolling rounds, moving slowly at the brink of dehydration, huffing out hopelessly in exhaustion, with nowhere to hide from the blazing sun, and probably searching with eagerness for someone on whom to take their frustration. But, as there was nothing that required their involvement, they pressed on forward, past twelve pairs of shapely bare legs, for which they were pretending not to care, while glancing every now and then, filling their eyes and minds with images of exposed female flesh, taking their time, but moving in the name of duty nonetheless. When the sweating representatives of the Mighty arm of Law disappeared behind a sand dune, Youssef was able to relax and with him, Yasmine and her friends.

This is how it started, on a perfect summer day, walking side by side, in a silence filled with excitement, all the way to the café, where, in a terrace watching over the ocean, they sat on two wooden stools facing one another, separated by a very small square table, in such proximity that their senses felt heightened, their minds lost in whirlwinds of hopes and sweet expectations.

Left alone, they talked and wandered, unaware of the ticking of clocks, the passing of time, the jealous looks, the venomous eyes, the apprehension, their nervousness seeping through their pores, the uncertainty of Tomorrows, the loneliness of Yesterdays, the unfairness of life with its too many disparities, the scurvy waiter taking too long to check on them and take their order, the flashing of youth, the inevitability of death, the bodies that decay, the friends who betray, the malevolence that soils the purity of hearts, the disheveled server who finally arrives, the note pad and pen he holds in his hand, the damp and unclean apron he seldom washes, the pollution dumped in the seas, the mercury in fish, the poisons we breathe, drink and eat, the leaders who betray, the oppressed, the tortured, the used, the swindled, the murdered, the imprisoned, the victims of power and of greed, the liars, the bullies, the truth distorters, the racists, the sexists, the fear that turns Good into Evil, the Hmm, Would you like to place an order, the eternity it takes for the two Colas they order to arrive on a black plastic tray.

"What's your last name?"
"Berrada, and yours?"
"Jazil… Not as popular as Berrada."

"I like it though. It sounds more interesting than mine."

"I guess there aren't too many Jazils out there."

"That makes you sort of unique."

"Sort of."

"Where do you live?"

"Casa."

"So do I."

"No way… I thought you were from here."

"I hoped you weren't."

"Where in Casa?"

"Maarif, and you?"

"Eindiab. Not too far from the lighthouse."

"I've never been by the lighthouse."

"It's not that great of a neighborhood, but it's a very interesting place. I could give you a free tour."

"A free tour, with no hidden agendas?"

"Of course not. It would be a proper and very official tour."

"I'm tempted to believe that."

"You should."

"I love learning new things."

"Oh, it would be very new. I can promise you that."

"Where can I sign up?"

"Consider it taken care of."

"Wow, now that's service."

"And you haven't seen anything yet?"

"I hope so."

"Mr. Jazil, it is a pleasure doing business with you."

"Thank you, Mss. Berrada. Your wish is my command."

"My personal genie, I don't know what to say…"

"Don't say anything then."

"Not a word?"

"Not a word. Unless you wish to speak, of course."

"Of course…"

"Did I tell you that I like your smile?"

"Wait a second. I thought there were no hidden agendas."

"Seriously, I do like your smile."

"It sounds like one those clichés, I would say, ninety nine percent of the global male population use on every girl they happen to come across."

"I don't know about the rest of the global male population. But your smile…"

"What about my smile, young man?"

"Well, how can say this?"

"Oh, I'm sure you can do it. But, I would say, it definitely has to be original."

"Well, then, here it comes. It's… how can I explain it…"

"Come on, I'm dying to hear it."

"It's magically uplifting."

"Magically uplifting…"

"You heard this one before. You did, didn't you?"

"Not really. But tell me, what else do you like?"

"You're not shy, are you?

"Is that a problem?"

"No, I actually like that about you too."

"Good. And what else?"

"Give me a second. I'm just getting to know you."

"Don't be shy now."

"I'm just saving the rest for later."

"Can I tell you what I like about you?"

"I'd love that?"

"I like your dimples."

"A lot of people like them. When I was a little kid, like three or four, I remember women grabbing me by the cheeks and pulling on them while screaming, 'Aren't his dimples cute!' So please, don't pull on my cheeks."

"How is your lip?"

"Tender, other than that, it feels okay."

"I'm sorry about the fight, I feel very responsible."

"Don't. It would have happened regardless. It's definitely not your fault."

"I was worried you wouldn't come back."

"I was afraid you would run away."

Gently, she pressed her cold bottle on his swollen lip. He grimaced but didn't pull back or stop smiling. A light glistened deep in his eyes, it made her blush and look at her hand. When she looked back up and found him, they both laughed and went back to talking.

"You should go see a doctor, it doesn't look very good."

"A doctor? No, it will heal in a couple of days."

"I wouldn't take any chances with a bruise that size."

"I'll be alright."

"You don't have to act tough to impress me."

"I'm not acting."

"So, you're a tough guy?"

"What do you think?"

"Well, if you really want my honest opinion, I'd say you're either tough or crazy, which of the two it is, I don't know you well enough to tell."

"Sounds like a problem that requires solving."

"I didn't say that."

"But you meant it."

"You're so full of yourself it makes me want to laugh."

"Go ahead laugh. I'll probably enjoy it very much."

"You know, after second thought, you are definitely crazy... Big time crazy."

"You're hurting my feelings. I'm about to start crying."

"Do you want to leave?"

"Not at all, I'm having too much of good time."

"That's good."

"Yes, it's better that good."

"So, what school do you go to?"

"Lycee Majd."

"Where is that at?"

"Not too far from the old Medina."

"I have never heard of it."

"I can include that in the tour."

"Sure. I would love that."

"Where do you go?"

"Lycee Chaouki, do you know it?"

"Who doesn't, all the pretty girls go there."

"Oh yeah?"

"That's what I hear."

"Sure."

"What?"

"I bet you went there a few times to pick up girls."

"Never!"

"Why not, don't you like pretty girls?"

"I …do. It just happens that your school is too far and I don't have time for running after pretty girls."

"Why?"

"I am just very busy."

"Doing what?"

"I go to school and practice football everyday."

"What year are you in?"

"Last."

"Me too."

"What are you going to do after you graduate?"

"Well… my father wants me to study economics; you see, he is a public accountant at the Ministry of finance."

"My father works there as well."

"Now that's a coincidence; and what does he do?"

"He's the… Ah, it's not important."

"Come on, I told you what mine does, you have to tell me."

"I do?"

"Yes Yasmine, yes, that's the rule."

"Really?"

"Come on, how about I let you pull on my cheeks if you tell me?" Come on."

"You would let me do that? You promise?"

"I Promise."

"Well… he's the minister."

"The minister?"

"The minister."

"Wow, that's something."

"How about your mom?"

"She's home. Does yours work?"

"Yes, she sews kaftans and all kinds of other dresses too. She's very good at it too. Do you have any brothers and sisters?"

"No, I'm an only child. How about you?"

"I have an older brother."

"How old is he?"

"Nineteen. Two years older than me."

"We're the same age then."

"What month were you born in?"

"December, and you?"

"May."

"What day?"

"The eighteenth."

"The sixteenth."

"You're almost six months older than I am."

"You must be top of your class in math."

"Your sarcasm reminds me of something…"

"Is it something good?"

"I would say: yes."

"What is it?"

"Your cheeks, I want to pinch them."

"Oh, that. I was hoping you wouldn't remember."

"I almost did. Now, remember your promise and lean closer, will you?"

"Here, have them; they're all yours."

"Thank you."

Yasmine and Youssef went on chatting, playing at getting to know each other, past the empty bottles, the stained glasses, and the laden ashtrays that had to be taken away by the waiter with a disenchanted face. They sat and listened to each other's voice, past the bill that was placed face down, the many patrons who came, sat and left, the suspiciously unsanitary rag used to wipe off the abandoned tables as soon as they were vacated. They talked for hours about silly subjects and somewhat more important matters. Until undeniably, they both felt the breeze, cold and pressing, demanding that they leave and seek the sun and its warming rays.

By then, the waiter had disappeared inside. When he returned, they had both left the premises. With utmost celerity, he moved to the table they had been occupying and collected the few bills and coins that were awaiting his arrival. Pausing for a second, he performed a quick mental calculation separating gratuity from bill. He put his share in one of his pants' pockets, and the employer's in his apron's. The moment stretched, so much that, unusually and instead of going on with his chores, he glanced at the empty chairs.

A fleeting image crossed the waiter's disillusioned mind, awakening dormant thoughts and abnegated wishes. He felt bitterness spread up his throat carried along by the resurfacing of a thousand silenced dreams. He remembered his longing for a caring woman, home cooked meals -filling and rich, and a soft bed, all at once. A couple walked in. He shrugged off all the unwanted feelings of sorrow and loss that had suddenly escaped his will and invaded his head and heart. He then greeted the new patrons with a wave, smeared the table's surface with his dampened piece of abused cloth, glanced over the beach, saw Yasmine and Youssef walking side by side, closer than when they had arrived, and smiled, a sincere understanding smile.

Serenely lost in each other's presence, in the enchanting ease of their conversation, in the symphonic melody of rolling waves shifting sand and whistling wind, in the inherent beauty of gliding birds with outstretched wings, dancing leafy branches and unfolding foamy water. As one, they drifted with the breeze, to a more intimate space, where, out of sight from those who knew them, they sat on softly cushioning sand. Leaning closely towards each other, hands freely caressing and playing in the shapelessness of the granulated carpet supporting them, they connected through eyes that shimmered brightly with the luster of joy.

The sun was receding, drawn by the horizon, lighting up the shore. Its rays stretched to touch their skins and be reflected by their irises, as they remained contentedly encapsulated in the peacefulness of the moment, in a deep sense of unforced equanimity. Pleasurably, they indulged in the misty afternoon breeze, as it gently caressed their faces, and playfully passed across and around their bodies, inescapably interlacing itself —as if meaning to bind and join them.

They would have stayed there forever, had it been possible. They would have stayed, for leaving could not mean anything but putting an end to beauty, perfection, happiness, and peace. They would have stayed had the choice been theirs. Unfortunately, it wasn't. One of Youssef's teammates arrived running to tell him that the bus that would take them back home was about to take off, that he should hurry to get on it if he didn't want to remain stranded on the beach until the next day. Youssef sighed in despair. He looked at Yasmine who smiled understandingly.

"I don't want to leave," he confessed while watching his friend who had already started walking away. Then turning to her, he added, "What if I never see you again?"

"I promise you that we'll meet again," she replied, in a tone meant to convey nothing but a strong conviction, and then stood up.

Youssef got on his feet, found himself unable to hide how uneasy he actually felt, and asked, "When?"

Yasmine opened both her arms and gave him a warm hug. It was the first she had ever shared with a man, who hadn't been a close relative. She knew how inappropriately she was behaving, but that didn't matter, because holding him felt right. It made her skin tingle and her head spin with joy. She felt his body breathe against hers and wondered what he was thinking; and just as that question was to summon sentiments of embarrassment and uncertainty, Youssef wrapped his arms around her, as if to share the guilt, heighten the pleasure, and obliterate any awkwardness that might arise between them.

He held on to her, heat radiating from his chest, ready to melt and surrender to her closeness. He wished for what was happening to last for as long as he was allowed to breathe. Then, just as the finality of everything was about to awaken the demon of fear, she brought her lips very closely to his ear, and whispered, "Meet me at the Corniche, next Saturday, by the McDonald's at two o'clock.

We could take a walk along the beach, or pick a café where we could sit, talk and enjoy the fresh air."

Releasing him, she felt his hands slide down the sides of her arms and stop against her elbows. She wanted to kiss him right there and then. He wanted to kiss her the way couples do at the end of their first date in romantic American movies, but could not summon enough courage to do it. She took a step back. His eyes lingered on her, helplessly drawn by her ravishing beauty. He made her blush. She inhaled deeply, and tilted her head to the left the way she had always done whenever shyness took hold of her. His nostrils flared, as desires rushed through him and flooded his mind.

She felt a mild wind blowing gently against her back, as if pressing her to move forward and closer to him. She resisted and stood still. He felt the gentle breeze pick up momentum and intensify, blowing her soft and dark hair over her shoulders, and in his direction. She held on and refused to give in to the wind's intervention and to her own wishes; and just to show that she was in control, at least that day, she used both hands to brush and hold her rebellious hair. Then, she sighed and smiled. He felt breathless -never before had he witness a sight as beautiful as she. He shook his hand, struggling to leave, because letting go, even momentarily, was too hard.

"You have to go now," she pointed to his friend whose moving figure was receding in the distance.

"You better be there," he said walking backwards.

She laughed and exclaimed, "Don't you worry about that, just come. I'll be there."

Youssef shouted, "See you Saturday," and went off running to catch up with his friend, and his head racing through time, into a world of delightful possibilities, into dreams that should have no endings, past the circumstantial delays of reality, and into a Saturday he could not wait reaching.

Yasmine began walking back in the same direction, yet staying along the moving water line, which, every now and then, touched her feet and erased her footsteps, so that whenever she turned around she could not help finding a deep similarity between how the ebb and flow of water was erasing her footprints and the manner in which the events that had just transpired, were rendering every past disappointment her passionate heart had experienced obsolete. Love, she was feeling, had undeniably come.

Some say that love is a sweetly scented wind that comes uninvited and sweeps you off your feet. Some say that like a desert storm, it enters your life, your body, your mind, bursting through all of the walls you've built around you out of fear. Some describe it as liberating. Others see it as intoxicating, and even maddening. A mythical blaze, unleashed, it seeks the soul, enflames the heart, tearing through the skin of every irrelevant belief, every whimsical foundation.

Love, they say, is a fiery wind, the combined breath of a million and one djinn, a crusting wave, raised to the heavens, bent to meet the heart, spun and moved by a million and one angel.

Love, they say, is the dance of the Divine Spirit, the greatest lover who upon choosing you to bestow her gifts, cuts through you with the unforgiving sharpness of her lust stained daggers, separating the gross from the glorious, the weak from the courageous, the blind from the wise.

Divine alchemist, bowing to no one, feared by all, she turns you into ashes and offers your remains in a swift gesture, mastered since before the beginning of Time, to Life unrestrained, Passion unbridled. Then having closed a cycle, having achieved wholeness, spirit into Spirit, she once again retires into her background. But not for long, for the dance never stops, and the dancer never tires.

Yasmine and Youssef met, as agreed, on Saturday, and from that day on, they sought each others' company as often as they could. They met to talk about no particular subject, and to walk to no particular destination. Being together, always sufficed, as they wandered through the bustling background of their labyrinthine city, each step, and each word bringing them closer, and closer, toward each other, until, unable to resist any longer, their hands managed to reach and touch.

Slowly, their fingers fanned out and interlaced, igniting the warmest of feelings, pleasurably palpable sensations that started spreading over the skin, running up and down the spine, to the brain, bursting like fireworks in a cloudless night sky, then cascaded down, all the way, to the toes and erupting back up to finally enter and swell the heart with marvelous joy.

"You never told me what you wanted to be."

"I don't know, my mother says either a pharmacist, a doctor, or a lawyer."

"But what do you want?"

"I have always wanted to play the guitar and sing."

"You know how to play the guitar?"

"Yes, I've been taking classes and practicing for twelve years now."

"You must be very good then."

"I'm okay."

"I want to hear you play."

"I'll have to bring my guitar with me then."

"When?"

"I don't know… sometime next week."

"I can't wait."

"How about you?"

"Do you play any instrument?"

"Well… I've never taken any classes, or anything like that, but I'm pretty good with the tahrija."

"That's not the same."

"What do you mean it's not the same? It's an instrument, isn't it?"

"Yes, but it's still not the same."

"I don't understand why you're laughing."

"Well… it's a tahrija."

"Exactly! A tahrija!"

"That's what I'm saying."

"Oh, I see."

"You think it's not a serious instrument. Well, allow me to educate you on the subject. The tahrija, which you happen to be mocking, is actually, and undoubtedly, a classical instrument, perhaps the ancestor of the drum."

"Sure."

"You can laugh all you want, it won't change the fact that I am in demand, yes, in demand, at weddings and such, for the extraordinary talent I display when holding the very instrument you are disrespecting."

"Stop! I beg you. You're killing me. I can't breathe."

"Go on laugh, one day I'll show you how good I make it sound and, then, you'll beg me to take you under my wing and teach you how to play it."

"How about I teach you to play cords and you teach me how to tap on a goat's skin or, even better, we could form a band and travel the world to entertain the masses."

"You'll have to be nicer first."

"Oh, I will."

"We'll have to see about that."

When September arrived and school had to be resumed, they both got busier, but still managed to find time to meet and be together. During those days, Youssef often studied, then worked at bettering his football skills, and finally raced, on the bicycle he borrowed from his brother, through Casablanca and its congested traffic, just to spend a few moments drinking from that heavenly cup of passion which Yasmine always eagerly offered him with an open heart. Enamored, they sat in backstreets and alleyways, sheltered within the shadows of old and silent trees, talking and holding hands, each minute shared sweeter than the sweetest fruit in the Garden of Eden.

Otherwise and whenever she could, Yasmine took a cab to Youssef's neighborhood to watch him practice. She would bring her guitar and start playing, so that soon enough, her presence at the edge of the football field became quite the attraction, as word got around about the young girl whose guitar filled the dusty arena with wonderful notes that always seemed to blend exquisitely into the most uplifting of tunes.

Soon enough more people started showing up during the football training sessions. They came in groups and alone. Kids, wondering couples, curious elders, and anyone who didn't have much to do -the last group being the largest, with unemployment and poverty rampant in that side of town. They sat around her in a circle, close enough to hear her play, but far enough so as not to make her uncomfortable, although the unoccupied space never remained so for long. Children, in their most uninhibited playfulness, always turned it to a stage of their own, as they played, danced, spun and ran around her, their obvious joy an inspiration for the very sound that was giving them wings with desires to fly.

Thus the performances went on until the athletes, their training over, stopped running and kicking the round ball. At that exact moment, Yasmine always put down her guitar, prompting the gathered spectators to give a round of applause before dispersing and leaving her alone so quickly that she sometimes wondered if they had actually been there at all, or if they were figments of her imagination. Whatever the case, she always felt grateful that there weren't any people around once Youssef came to join her.

In the privacy provided by the emptying stadium, and with those who might judge and condemn no longer there, the couple sought closeness and intimacy, in a tender ritual which always began with Yasmine usually opening a bag and pulling out a few plastic containers full of homemade culinary wonders she had brought for her dedicated athlete to try and hopefully enjoy. Lost in intimacy, they shared food Adil had never tasted and -sometimes- never heard of, dishes so rich and tasteful they made him moan, each time they found his palate, a reaction that never failed to bring a smile to her face, followed by a "What are you laughing at?" face out of him, and a "Nothing, you just make me want to feed you everyday,' sort of grin.

In those days, it was as if Love and Music were imbuing everything that could be met by the senses. Yasmine carried her guitar wherever she went, and played whenever she could. Sitting on a chair, a bench, bolder, or grass, and sometimes even leaning against the plainest of walls, holding the instrument against the right side of her ribcage and on top of the thigh of a raised and bent right leg, Yasmine played and played, her fingers moving and picking with, either, moving softness, or unbelievable lightness and celerity. Tapping on the ground with her left heel, body rocking, and eyes closed, she let her fingers run, and run, as if possessed by the very desire to create sound after sound, telling a story made with musical notes, losing herself to whatever rhythm had been seeking her body.

In moments like those, the passersby and meanderers always stopped and gathered around her, some nodding their appreciation and admiration for the displayed talent, others clapping along and stomping with their feet, which made her smile and often blush, but never stop playing. Her notes suffused the air and caused the faces of those present to soften as they gazed with dreamy eyes, their senses drawn to her -the unexpected musician who captured their inspirations.

Often one could hear their voices, as comments were exchanged, "She's amazing." They would nod and predict, "Someday she'll become a world known artist," or, "Let me tell you, a few years from now she'll be giving concerts and appearing on the most popular television variety shows," along with questions that didn't require answers, "Isn't she something else? Can you believe your ears?" and, "I mean… have you ever heard a sound as inspiring and uplifting as the one that comes from her guitar?"

Yasmine, on the other hand, never thought of it that way. No, for her, playing was the most natural and spontaneous activity she could lose herself in. And if one were to ask her about her sentiments regarding potential fame and apparitions on the national television station, her reply would have, probably, been one that conveyed that the only certainty she carried within was knowing that whenever she began playing life appeared to seize moving about in its usual randomness. It was as if the whole world was attuning itself to the notes her fingers were drawing out of the instrument's strings. In such moments, problems, in their largeness and smallness, disappeared and everything was just right, and that made her feel at peace within. Playing her guitar made her happy, and didn't someone say that happiness didn't have a price.

Happiness made life taste sweeter; and with Youssef around, it did so tenfold, especially, once Yasmine began teaching him how to play a few notes, and to her amazement, his hands and fingers caught on very, very quickly. Malleable and eager to impress, he strived toward mastery, so that soon enough they started playing music for each other, sharing sounds inspired by passion, building melodies sweet enough to leave a lingering pleasant mark as they dissolved in the open air.

Sharing one instrument, they played outside, and didn't care about what others might say or think. One could often spot them, sitting by the lighthouse, or on one of the benches scattered inside the public park of the city center, or on one of those stands surrounding the dusty soccer stadium Youssef trained in after school. They would be there facing each other, their heads almost touching, as they passed each other the guitar, in bonding complicity, trying to capture the rhythm of some song, tweaking it here and there, sometimes clapping, or even drumming on the hollowed instrument, inspiration and love their obvious and only guides.

Yasmine and Youssef couldn't get enough of each other. Intimacy was undoubtedly an addiction they could not and would not resist, for they were both aware of the precariousness of their situation. How long could they hide their union from the parents? How long could they go on playing hide and seek with the grim face of possible separation? The idea of being separated made them ache with anticipation for these reunions they managed to steal from their structured lives, over and over again, despite the semi-secrecy their burning relationship had to be built upon, the constant fear that their families might find out, and the disapproving culture and tradition to which they both belonged.

United in the forbidden, the shunned upon, feeling oppressed by the world, they could only find peace in each other's presence. It was as if they needed each other to recognize the sweetness in the pulse of life running through their awakened flesh. It was as if nothing and no one could keep them apart, not strangers frowning at their behavior, not even the prowling police always on the lookout for unwedded couples, sinners committing acts of public indecency and embracing immorality, to arrest and fine.

Daring the world and breaking laws erected in the sanctity of their land's history, risking more than anyone ought to risk, Yasmine and Youssef even managed to meet on the weekends, despite the difficulty of coming up with convincing excuses and alibis to cover their tracks, taking advantage of the complicity of some of Yasmine's abating girlfriends, who, in their strategic eagerness to participate in trysts, never refused to be part of any cover up operation that might come their way.

On those days and with more time at hand, the lovers sometimes retreated into the privacy of an empty warehouse, which Youssef had discovered a way to access. There, they could have a good time, out of sight, as she tried to teach him how to dance the merengue, the mambo, and even, when she felt inspired enough, the tango, through hours filled with music coming out of a tiny portable boom box, and sweet arguments born between patience and frustration, and laughter at his inability to avoid being a nervous dancer.

But if the weather was warm enough, then they usually preferred to make their way past the light house, across the construction sites and through the slum, all the way to the rocky cliff overseeing the ocean —their ocean. There, they used to sit on their favorite bolder, and, watch young boys clad in cheap swim trunks standing atop one of the most popular diving spots in the area, a mere rocky protrusion, some twenty meters above sea level, taking turns to jump into the shore's unsettled spume, arms spread open, chests expanded, gliding through empty space, as if daring the world and its countless limitations, turning to, and for just a second or two, amazing daredevils, curved bodies suspended in midair, aiming for the foamy water awaiting them below, to penetrate with utmost grace and skill, like flying arrows meant to be completely swallowed by the ocean.

With each jump, Yasmine tightened her grip around Youssef's arm praying for the diver to be one of the lucky ones who emerged without a scrape out of that shallow basin of unsettled water, under which hid the treacherous razor-like-teeth of a blood thirsty unforgiving bottom. She held her breath in anticipation, until the foolish boy reappeared again, and always waited for a proof that the thrill-seeking juvenile was still alive, to exhale in relief, and lean forward to better assess how much damage was caused by the shear carelessness and utter boredom of adolescence. Then and finally, she either bit her lower lip and let out an emphatic shiver, or smiled and pressed Youssef's arm with her hand, relief and excitement overwhelming her naturally calm nature, as she watched the fortunate diver climb back up the tall rocky cliff to rejoin his friends and celebrate.

It was there, not too far from the construction sites and the slum, on the rocky cliff overseeing the ocean, on that very bolder they had claimed as their own, that Yasmine and Youssef first kissed. It happened under a bright blue sheltering sky, and in front of a glossy breathing ocean. Youssef had just finished carving the outline of a heart containing both their names, using a chisel borrowed from his brother —who was studying to be a wood carver and carpenter. They began talking almost as usual. But then, one word instead of leading to another, led to silence.

Suddenly, it was as if speech had been rendered meaningless, as if all words had been exhausted, as if all sounds had to be set aside. A wave of silence rose, spread and swallowed everything around them, leaving them nowhere to escape. They were breathing the hushed breath of inevitability, their longing for each other feeling unbearably magnified, and their senses painfully heightened to the point of becoming unbearable. Inescapably, Yasmine and Youssef became lost in each other's eyes, and neither one could quell the overwhelming intensity of attraction, the rawness of their binding desires.

They were burning from within, and with them every rule of conduct set forth by tradition and culture, every bylaw set to prevent them from falling into moral sin, impropriety and disgrace. They were burning in a blaze of passion their devouring eyes couldn't quench.

Inevitably, Yasmine's hand reached, sliding through both space and time, through what was permissible and what wasn't, and touched his. Youssef inhaled deeply while every fiber of his being felt her emancipating caress. Breeching through guilt, as well as through fear, they got a little closer, guided by the hypnotic throbbing of wildly untamed hearts beating too fast, then too slow, consciousness awaiting to find ecstasy, suspended on the tips of their slightly parted and glowing lips.

Beyond them, the world seized existing, as their breaths intertwined. Their eyes closed and their lips touched. A wave crashed on a rock breaking into a million droplets that spread, carried by the wind like mist, to spray their faces. A boy reemerged out of the water, unscathed. With a smile meant for the heavens, he looked up and found them kissing and holding onto each other in a gentle embrace. The diver thought about shouting something funny and clever, but for some reason beyond his understanding, he decided not to interrupt. He turned around and started swimming, leaving them lost in tenderness, breathing in, breathing out, bound by passion, their hearts ablaze, in love.

Their last high school year was one unlike the others, filled with group studies in terraces of cafes bordering Casablanca's main public park among new and old friends, around tables laden with blossoming ashtrays filled with twisted cigarette butts, empty bottles, stained espresso cups, transparent glasses marked with red lipstick prints, and warm brass teapots, with music uninterruptedly spilling out of cheap speakers hung on large and familiar pine trees, a cool breeze, leafy swaying branches, friendly tiny birds picking at crumbs around their feet, refreshing jokes, care-free laughter, and meaningful, yet subtly placed, glances.

It was a year brightened by love, sweetened by passion, enriched with political discussions, philosophical debates, enlightening literature, uplifting prose and daring theater productions. Above all, it was the best year of their lives. It began with the wind shifting from pleasant to invasively cold, and the sky's color fluctuating between blue and gray on a daily basis.

September was concluding its reign, making room for the very first rains, the ones that left the city's pavement slippery, wet and streaked with oil stains. As was its habit, the month of Virgo, while making room for Libra, was calling out boys and girls, children and teenagers, dressed for school, and carrying backpacks or cheap briefcases, into a continuously morphing urban structure, during the impossibly frustrating rush hours, to be herded in throngs inside grim looking buildings supposedly designed to provide the grounds for educating the masses, molding and shaping the future, creating the leaders and workers of tomorrow —goals, which many a critic have been heard pointing, at the risk of sounding belligerent toward those in charge of the proverbial stick and carrot, remain very far from being achieved.

Once again, Autumn was claiming Casablanca's five districts and affecting their communities, as it moved through its courts, streets, avenues, boulevards and neighborhoods disregarding all man-made lines of demarcation, oblivious to the importance and relevance of all the socio-cultural statuses and differences regulating that citizenry's lives.

The rainy season's arrival was, as it had for time unspoken, erasing the inescapable routine that is so characteristic of Summer. Autumn brought along change, freshness and an abundance of possibilities. It made life move to a more determinedly sounding beat and pace, or at least with less hesitancy. It pressed school attendants to lock the doors of their governmentally run establishments, allowing for old friendships to be rekindled, and new ones to be born. Autumn offered reasons and excuses for time to be spent away from home, when the young and restless neither had the desire nor the patience to stay home.

But most importantly, Autumn inspired couples, just like Yasmine and Youssef, to go on warmth-seeking walks, along familiar winding path that sluiced through parks full of tall whispering trees, between shielding shadows and comforting light, on crackling carpets of dry leaves and pine cones, sharing a purchased cone of roasted sunflower seeds or deep fried and sugar-coated chouro ringlets, so that by the time Winter showed up, having established their routines, could adjust more easily to the rain doubling in intensity, as well as to the cold and damp days the new season was pushing forth.

Thus, as the sun was concealed by ominously dark

clouds, they hid inside cafes and among others like them, ordered tea or coffee, and, talked for hours. They went to cinemas, not to watch movies, but to hide and kiss and caress each other, two anonymous silhouettes lost in the dark. Winter or no winter, they had each other, and that was enough to brighten their days, no matter how overcast.

Then Spring arrived, bright and colorful, laden with beautiful gifts that turned to moments full of furtive kisses in alleyways and behind shrubs, of rendezvous in the back rows of cinemas, of every social wrong feeling oh-so-right, of taboos discreetly embraced, of flesh seeking as well as beseeching, and of privacy in a meekly furnished apartments on the third floor of some old and bland looking building on a very quiet street near Yasmine's school, where, despite the burden of guilt, they learnt to surrender to each other, wrapped in semi-darkness, discovering and revealing themselves to each other.

But even spring had to leave. It had to bid them farewell, and when it did, they were there, standing on the shoreline, not too far from the construction sites and the slum, on the rocky cliff overseeing their ocean. She was in his arms, and he was in her heart. He glistened in her eyes and she inspired his breath.

They were standing there, in love, lost in each other, in joy and bliss, as Summer closed in and saw their spirits rising as one, transcending beyond the brightness of the sun, the vastness of the sky and the impalpability of the horizon. There, a warm breeze, carrying the scent of everything that had been and still was, reached and touched them. It blew like a blessing along the softness of their union, kindling the bright flame that was born to their love. It came as a lingering caress, a gift from the Divine. Circling their union, it held them at the center of everything, and as a witness, was there to hear a promise freely and willingly shared, below the bluest of skies, the brightest of suns, in utmost truthfulness, between two surrendering hearts, for this was what they both desired the most, a promise to never let go of their love.

A few weeks later, in the beginning of sunny July, at a time between the end of the school year and the release of its academic final results, Yasmine was flouncing down the streets of a city she knew and loved, on her way to meet with destiny, gracefully moving on the balls of her feet, as if too light to remain on the ground, dancing to the rhythm of unrestrained passion, transported by the breeze.

It was then that she saw him, standing at a street corner, right next to a rusty stop sign, his hands in his pockets, his head down, as if lost in thought, as if focusing on the little section of side-walk caught between his shoes.

"Hi you…" she had missed him and could not wait to hold him in her arms. Youssef looked up. She barely recognized his face, so much it looked different, so much it seemed disfigured with either pain or anger. His eyes, burning with the color of hate pierced her with fear.

"What's wrong?" she slowed down a few meters away from him, slowly surrendering to a presentiment warning her that she was heading to a catastrophe she could not fathom.

"I don't want to see you again," he glowered.

The abhorrent words he suddenly uttered penetrated her with the coolness of deadly venom. She stared at him unable to speak, chilled with doubt and uncertainty.

"Whatever you imagined was between us is over," his voice sounded cuttingly crisp, as if sharpened by rage.

"What are you talking about?" Yasmine was falling into the void that had cruelly opened up beneath her feet, "Are you mad?"

"I don't want to see you again," he was breathing as if possessed by a demon, "I hate you!"

In despair, she heard herself silently praying he would stop. In loss, she saw herself believing they could pretend that nothing was said. In agony, she convinced herself that she could erase it all out of her head, "Youssef, please what is wrong with you?"

"I told you, it's over." He turned around and walked away.

"Youssef..." she reached out with her hand and grabbed him from his right arm, but his arm tensed and was wrenched violently out of her desperate, but, weak grip.

Overtaken by what could only be rage, he turned to face her and shouted, "It's over."

His devastating words, like a spear that had been dipped in a deadly concoction, hit her in the chest and pierced her heart. She froze, as the shrilling poison took hold of her body. Helpless, too hurt and lost to stop him, she watched him leave.

Yasmine started praying, praying for the wheels of time to stop, spin the opposite way, erase what was unfolding, and give them a second chance. Yasmine prayed with tears in her eyes. She prayed with a wounded heart. But Youssef never stopped, never turned back. He kept on bearing down with his hands in his pockets.

Falling into an abyss whose existence she could not have imagined a minute ago, she desperately called his name three times, but Youssef never looked back. He pressed on, inescapably turning to a disappearing figure in the painfully growing distance, until all that was left, along with the sun caressing her skin, was a persistent wind still carrying his fragrance, still playing with her dress, still blowing through her hair.

It was on that day that Yasmine started hating the wind, the sun and anything that reminded her of him; the wretched man who broke her heart; the man she can't help but loathe.

Not too far from walled-in wealthier neighborhoods, across forgotten construction sites and the slum that had somehow managed to grown and spread along a section of Casablanca's precious shoreline, not too far from the light house, in front of a cliff overlooking the ocean, a few steps away from a boulder on whose smoothly eroded surface is carved the outline of a heart containing two names, a modestly dressed gray-haired woman sits on a bench. She's there watching a little child who is, in front of her, playing in a field of boulders, picking up pebbles to throw as far as his arm allows. There is much affection in her eyes. There is much sadness in her heart.

The boy waves at his grandmother and starts running toward her. She opens her arms with a welcoming smile. She leans forward and calls him in with both hands. When, suddenly, a cool and gentle breeze pulls at the scarf covering her hair. The breeze, strangely sweet scented, caresses her face while filling the space between her opened palms. Her world for a second seems to pause, Time lingering suspended, the air surrounding her vividly palpable. Distracted, she's shaken by the sudden impact caused by a little devil landing on her chest. She looks down and finds her little angel. His laughter floods her world and clears her mind of everything else. She laughs back, her heart flooded with love.

She hugs him. He wriggles gently out of her grip, jumps down, kisses her hands and runs back to his rocky playground. With the boy gone again, she's left alone, staring at the center of her palm, where Adam's lips had lovingly landed with softness, and where a curtain of memories was cruelly opening up, exposing old hidden wounds. A warm smile she yearns for. The beautiful face of a child she would give her life to touch again. He too used to hold her hand and kiss it on the palm, just like her grandson had done. She hadn't seen her son for ten long years.

She sighs and closes her eyes trying, if only for a moment, to forget. But, as it is sometimes, memories have a mind of their own. Sometimes they lead you, whether you like it or not, to those very places one is desperately trying to avoid.

Thus, sitting on her bench, she surrenders to the image of a baby boy, so fragile, so bold, his eyes seldom opened, his fingers and toes so small. She hears the first sounds he makes and then the first words he manages to utter. She sees him crawling on both hands and knees. She sees his first attempts at walking as well as his first successful steps. The baby becomes a child who loves kissing his mother's hands and cheeks. He runs all the time, often following a ball he never tires from kicking.

She sees the boy who could do no wrong, the boy with the most generous heart, loving and caring, and who, no matter what he has done, has to be forgiven because of that big, genuine, smile that always shines between his two adorable dimples.

She aches, as memories of her baby boy turn to those of a young man, inspired by larger than life dreams, dedicated to his goals. He wanted to be a professional football player, and believed he could. She sees him dream and hears him say how he would buy his mother a very big house in the nicest part of town, but not too far from the ocean, because he knows the shore makes her happy. A house with enough maids she wouldn't have to do anything but relax and enjoy herself. His father would retire and get the break he deserves. They would eat meat, chicken and fish whenever they fancied. He would open a shop for his brother to prosper and show the world what a talented carpenter he is. He would help everyone in the neighborhood. He would open up a club where all the poor kids would be able to play for free. His dreams strike her, one by one, vividly, strongly, and, oh so painfully.

She wishes she could think of something else. Anything. Seagulls circling in the sky, clouds weightlessly hovering above, Adam jumping from boulder to boulder, but the visions persist. They fill her mind, demanding her unequivocal attention. She tries to resist, but to no avail. The young man sits at the dinner table, along with his father and older brother. She's there too. She hears him speak of a girl he's met, while devouring a buttered slice of homemade bread and drinking a hot cup of spearmint tea. There is so much exhilaration in her voice. She hears him say, with no explanation, that one day even a political figure, a minister of finance, would be impressed and honored if he –the football star and national hero- were to ask for his daughter's hand. His brother laughs at the comment. His father, eyes suddenly ablaze, tells them that he hopes that no son of his is seeing a girl without her parents' consent. Her son nods his head in silent acquiescence. He lowers his eyes to look at his plate and goes back to finishing the meager meal his family was able to afford that night.

Then she's alone with him in the kitchen. He's helping her with the dishes while humming one of her favorite songs. She looks at him and smiles. Her baby boy is now a young man, much taller than she, healthy and strong. He could probably lift her off of the ground if he wanted.

He has grown, yet in her eyes he still remains her precious little boy. Yes, in those motherly eyes of hers, he hasn't changed at all. Or, perhaps he has, she looks again, and notices something very different about him, something she should have seen a long time ago. It is the girl. She can see her. She can see her in his eyes, in his expressions, in his features, and in his every action. In fact, she can even feel her presence in and around him. And there, she sees herself wanting to say something –but what can she possibly say that would change his mind? No, it is an experience he has to go through on his own, a lesson to learn. And so, she chooses to remain silent.

Today, she believes he is alive. No, she doesn't believe. She knows. She knows because of the checks from abroad, the ones the postman drops every three months, or so. She knows he is there, surely doing well, how else would he be able to send her all that money on a regular basis? Yes, there are ways; she's heard about them. Young desperate men who leave their countries, their families and friends, lured by the West and the riches it brandishes at their faces, through the television screen, the cinema, the songs that are played on the radio, and all those foreign magazines that are sold at every corner kiosk. She's heard about the sons of mothers just like herself who hide inside freight ships, bargaining their lives, hoping to survive the crossing of the Mediterranean waters, for some don't, hoping not to be caught, arrested and deported.

Good sons, full of potential, go where they do not belong, dreaming of finding work, and maybe a little dignity, money to buy things, a chance to spread happiness back home with expensive gifts, second hand items -of course, but who cares and who would know? Not those who receive them. Not those who dream they could do the same. She's heard about those poor souls, and even knows a few. They go where they are not welcome. They go with so much potential, carrying so many dreams and hopes, carrying the weight of all the relatives who are awaiting their call so that they too may follow in their footsteps, there, where the grass is greener, where cars are cheaper, and where is money seems to fall from the trees.

Disillusioned sons, laden with hopes, go seeking all the things they've been denied, only to be handed more misery than they've ever known, as contrast between having and not having heightens their pain and deepens their despair. And, soon enough, with a concession here, and another there, they change, eaten from within. They forget who they are, dropping honor and all, allowing hunger and greed to guide their actions and deeds. They become criminals, prostitutes, thieves or drug dealers. They make money, but it all disappears as quickly as they touch it, for what is gathered wrongfully can never bear fruit. Eventually, we harvest what with our hands we planted.

Nadia shakes her head, trusting that her son, Youssef would never do such a thing. No, not Youssef… She closes her eyes and wishes him well, for that is all she can do, while waiting for a word, a phone call, a letter, or even a visit. She imagines him knocking at the door. What a blessing, what a joyful day, and the questions he would answer, and the laughter they would have. Not today though, she sighs. Maybe tomorrow. Maybe tomorrow…

Sitting on the bench, heavily burdened with regret, with sadness for what has befallen her family, she feels the warmth of tears running down her cheeks. She wipes them off slowly with the palms of her hennaed hands. She gives in to her sorrow and to the bitterness of her own memories, as they take her to a very dark day, a little more than ten years ago. There was fabric, red as blood, moving underneath her hands, the sound of her sewing machine, mechanical, familiar, and a maroon dashed-line stretching over soft crimson silk. Then, there was a knock at her shop's door. It was ten after ten. She got up and opened her door to find a woman she had never seen before.

"Hello," said the stranger dressed in expensive imported clothes no one the seamstress knew could ever afford. The sparkling jewels on the unexpected visitor's neck, ears and wrists seemed to draw in all the fading daylight that was reaching the building's corridor, to immediately reflect it in bright colorful filaments stretching and shimmering in every direction, before dissolving as if absorbed by the radiant softness of the visitor's ageless face, the depth of her piercing green eyes, and the glistening of her immaculately long and wavy golden hair.

"May I come in? I would like to speak with you," her voice sounded clear, unrestrained, untouched by fear or modesty.

"Of course, come on in… but excuse me if I don't recognize you," she stepped aside and smiled respectfully, "You must be here to place an order?" There was uncertainty in her voice, as she knew very well that that type of woman would never be interested in ordering anything from a modest seamstress such as herself. In fact, she could swear that a woman, as obviously rich and distinguished as this one standing in front of her, never sat foot in her impoverished part of town.

"Thank you," said the elegant stranger smiling coldly. Then, graciously she walked in, filling the room with the sweet scent of a very light and pleasant perfume, "Actually, I'm not here to order a dress from you."

The seamstress closed the door, while keeping her eyes on this perplexing guest who had now stopped in the middle of the room, in an opaquely lighted space beyond which everything else was blending in the darkness of foggy shadows.

"In fact, we do not know each other and we have never met." Slowly, she waved her hand, as if to dismiss what she had just said, and perhaps because it was too obvious and unimportant, "What brings me here is your son."

The mother nodded, "Oh, I see," then she walked to her work station, pushed some opened boxes away from a four legged wooden chair to offer it to the worrisome visitor, "Please, have a seat."

"Thank you," the stranger examined the chair with a quick glance before taking a seat, "By the way, my name is Amina."

"And I am Nadia," she took a deep breath and sat down by her old black sewing machine.

"Nadia, you seem to be a wise woman," Amina spoke calmly, while her bright eyes took in the place, "I have the feeling we will understand each other."

"What can I do for you, Madame?" Unconsciously, Nadia interlaced her fingers and rested her hands over thighs she was nervously pressed together.

"A favor, I hope. Actually, a favor for the both of us.

You see, your son has been seeing my daughter, secretively, without our permission —or your knowledge, I assume, for a while now. I just found out about it two days ago." Her smile was fading and with it, the softness of her features. Her gaze became one of clear determination and control, "I figured I would come to let his parents know about his unacceptable behavior, so that they would intervene and put a stop to his disastrously thoughtless actions, and that, hopefully before my dear husband finds out."

Amina's eyes slanted as she flared her nostrils, "Because, if he ever finds out, and I hope for everyone's sake that he doesn't, things will get out of hand, and, I assure you that many will have to pay for your son's irresponsible behavior." Then leaning forward, she sighed, "I am sure you see and understand how sensible this matter is, for my family as well as for yours. My daughter's honor is at stake, and my dear husband, although a very kind and forgiving man, is extremely intransigent when it comes to the honor of his only daughter."

Her voice had become so chillingly threatening it removed any hint of benevolence from her appearance, as she unwaveringly stared into the eyes of the cornered seamstress, "I realize that what I am telling you might come as a shocking revelation, but it is of the utmost importance that we keep our heads clear and act as swiftly as we can. Believe me. I am on your side. I really am…" as if enjoying the way the echo left by her words filled the entire room, Amina stopped talking and tilted her head, perhaps to better scrutinize Nadia with her probing eyes, before allowing the nuance of a smile and continuing, "if we take care of this aberration now, before it is too late, I promise you that a great deal of pain and humiliation will be avoided. My husband, you see, may God protect him, is a minister and his arm is far reaching. I am afraid that if he gets involved, your whole family might suffer and we don't want that; do we now, my dear?"

Nadia nodded. Sitting still, she took it all in, one word at a time, one stab at time, even when every word she was hearing came distorted, as if wrapped in the hiss of a serpent. She looked at Amina and saw no pity, no forgiveness, no compassion. She had lived long enough to read between the lines. She had seen her share of pain to know that a great deal of it was undoubtedly coming. "So is life," she thought.

"I assure you that you are very fortunate I have found out about this tragedy before he did. I am much more open-minded. I remember being their age once, incapable of discerning right from wrong. I remember being too young to see clearly into the future where the consequences of every choice made are surely awaiting. Our children, just as I was, are in a phase of their lives in which they are in a dire need for guidance," Amina paused allowing a sad grin to show on her face, "I am sure that your son is a nice young man. He just isn't the right young man for my daughter, wouldn't you agree?"

"Yes, I do," responded Nadia, sounding utterly disheartened. A heavy load had settled over her shoulders, pressing her down and onto her knees. It had broken her spirit. "How unfair this world is," she cried in silence. She heard the minister's wife ask her, "Will you help me Nadia?"

She wanted to answer and say, "Yes Madame, I will. Don't you worry, Madame; I will make sure that my undeserving son will never bother your precious daughter.

You can go back to your home, Madame; I will take care of everything once and for all. And please, please, please accept my deepest apologies, as well as that of my whole family, for all the trouble we have caused you." Nadia wanted to say every word she was supposed to say. She was ready to cry and bow down, ready to kiss those cold manicured hands, plead for forgiveness, and beg for mercy. But the cornered mother was not given a chance to speak as a tremulous male voice suddenly filled the room.

"She won't have to."

Both women looked toward the door and found Youssef standing, face twisted in anger.

"Youssef..." his mother stood up unable to hide her surprise.

Unfazed, Amina examined him calmly from her seat, "So, this is the source of our troubles. I have to say that I am pleased with my daughter's taste," she looked at Nadia and nodded, "I can almost see what attracted her to him." Her smile disappeared in the stealth of seriousness as soon as she brought her eyes back on Youssef, "However ..."

"Look, I heard what you had to say. You don't have to threaten anyone, and especially not my mother."

Amina listened airily, and as if unaffected by his apparent rage.

"Youssef please!" pleaded his mother.

"I will not be bothering your daughter anymore," he sounded furious, barely able to contain himself.

"Well, thank you Youssef. That is exactly what I came to hear," Amina's distinct voice was as calm as is it was clear.

Youssef grabbed the door that was still ajar and pushed it all the way against the wall, and held it there, "Since you've gotten what you came for, I would like you to get out of here now." He was breathing heavily.

Amina stood up with distinguished grace. She smiled at the seamstress who had turned worriedly pale and offered her a sort of amused look, all the while taking her time to acknowledge the young man's angry fit.

"And if there is anything else, regarding my person, you would like to discuss in the future, I would suggest you do it directly with me." Youssef spoke bitterly, waiting for her to turn around and look at him.

Still gazing at the seamstress, Amina replied, "I don't think we will need to discuss anything after this," she spun around and challengingly stared him in the eyes, "However, if I ever find out that you are still pursuing my daughter, it will not be me who gets involved. Understand?"

"Perfectly," he grunted, looking so tense and ready to lose control, clinging to the door and still forcibly pressing it against the wall.

"Well then, my work here is done. Nadia it was nice meeting you. I wish you all the luck with your…" she looked around her, "…little business here, and with such a hot-tempered child." Then, with a flourish of a hand, she started toward the opened door and Youssef.

"Yes," responded Nadia with a broken voice, "Have a nice day Madame. And sorry again for all the trouble we have caused you."

Youssef and his mother remained still as Amina walked out of the apartment, and into the building's hallway. They were looking at each other when Amina's nobly cold voice reached them, "As long as we could fix it." The sentence echoed in the room and in their ears. It echoed long after it was said, long after Amina had vanished, its meaning lingering even after the darkness of the coming night seeped through the windows, spread between the mother and her son as they sat, wrapped in gloom, in a room that had been robbed of its usual warmth and had become painfully desolate.

Nadia closes her eyes, then with the sleeves of her dress, wipes off tears she no longer cares to retain. She looks at the little boy, who is playfully throwing pebbles at the ocean, and smiles. She smiles despite the agony that fills her heart.

"If I didn't know better I would say that you're Basque," boasted Alberto, in the shadowy interior of a dimly lit Norwegian pub, after having gulped down half the content of a large pitcher of locally brewed beer.

Andalou laughed, "It probably has something to do with you talking in my ears when I am asleep."

The old sailor wiped his gray moustache dry with the back of his hand and said, "Sometimes, the end justifies the means."

Andalou frowned, "All I'm trying to say is that you should consider getting some sleep from time to time."

Alberto opened a cigarette box that was lying on the table, pulled out a cigarette, quickly put it between his lips, before lighting it using the silver lighter he religiously carried in his pocket, "Sleep is for those who need it, and at my age, I rarely do."

Andalou waved to the restlessly moving waitress, "… just let me know when you start seeing things."

The old man nodded, "You'll be the first informed."

"I have no doubt about that."

Alberto, leaned back on his chair, stretching his bulky torso, and winked at the plush woman in charge of re-plenishing their pitchers, "Be positive my friend, life is too short to be wasted in negativity."

"Who's negative?" asked the somewhat grim looking sailor, before ordering another round.

"You're kidding me, right?" Alberto clapped and add-ed, pointing at the cleavage hanging at arms reach from him, "Do you know what you need, son?"

Andalou smirked, "More beer."

"No. You need to a beautiful pair of breasts… a pair just like these."

"I'm very sorry…" Andalou looked apologetically at the tall and grimacing descendent of giant Valkeries.

"Sorry? You don't have to be sorry. We all know that I mean it as a compliment," Alberto grinned at the coldly staring waitress, before continuing, "boy, you must be crazy. When I was your age I would have been on them the way a mean dog would on a bone. What is wrong with you?"

Andalou shook his head. He looked at his only friend, and sighed.

"Seriously, how can you say no to such wonders of tenderness?" He pointed with both opened hands to his subject of admiration, totally oblivious to the impatient look he was getting from the face which came with the generously developed physique.

"I'm just not as obsessed by women as you are."

Alberto coughed a couple of times, crushed his cigarette, looked at their sighing hostess, apologized profusely on behalf of his friend who obviously was suffering from one of those youth's idealistic depressive bouts, then shaking his head, asked for another pitcher.

Then, leaning toward Andalou, he whispered, "How long has it been?"

"What are you talking about?"

"You know damn well what I am talking about…" Alberto sat an elbow on the table and pensively scratched his chin, "How long has it been since you… touched a woman?"

Andalou rapped with his fingertips on the table and replied, "I'm fine."

The old sailor stared at his friend and, raising a bushy

eyebrow, said, "Take my advice son, and seek the comfort of a woman before it's too late."

Andalou closed his eyelids, concealing what regret and sorrow his deep brown irises contained, "You know Alberto, for a wise old man, you're rather narrow minded."

Alberto chuckled and asked, "What else is there?"

Andalou laughed, shaking his head, and then replied, "I'll let you know when I find out."

Alberto closed his eyes, leaned back on his chair, and grinned, "You do that son. You do that…"

Tracing invisible spirals on the ground, a small and crumpled yellow candy wrapper passes in front of Nadia. A spurious wind pulls out strands of hair from underneath her head scarf. The wrapper stops and then goes on swirling by her feet. For a second, she is inspired to reach and grab it. But instead she undoes her scarf and fixes her hair. Eyes drawn to the moving piece of plastic, she watches it leave center stage, to be immediately replaced by an old looking fellow with deep and comforting eyes.

Offering an honest smile and speaking with an enjoyably foreign accent, he asks her if she doesn't mind sharing the bench. She replies that she certainly doesn't, while sliding to her right. He thanks her and takes a seat. They look at each other and smile, her shyly, him generously. She feels an unexpected wave of warmth rising within. Inexplicably, she wants to start talking to him. Finding her reaction rather odd, she diverts her eyes looking for the boy whom she finds, still busy throwing pebbles into the ocean, his legs straddling a dark rock twice his size.

The old man opens a green backpack, as old, torn and covered with stitched seams as the blue –fading to gray- vest he is wearing over a lighter, azure-blue, button-up cotton shirt and a pair of navy pants. He pulls a clear plastic bottle, uncaps it and, in that very soft and peculiar accent of his, offers the woman some water. She politely declines. He smiles, bringing the bottle, as well as her attention, closer to a face carved with possibly as many as a thousand wrinkles, each with a story to tell. Attracted by these lines left by time, Nadia's gaze lingers, wandering from one wrinkle to another, until she catches herself staring at the old man. Embarrassed, and unable to stop her face from blushing, she turns her gaze to her grandson.

"Beautiful day for watching a loved one play, isn't it?"

Nadia responds softly, very glad he's spoken to her, "Yes, a very beautiful day, indeed." She then glances at the old fellow and sees a kind profile, and a restive gaze lost over the ocean. Shyly, she lowers her eyes, but only to lift them again, this time finding a contented smile, and a look of obvious peace. A peace she can actually feel. A peace that she experiences as surrounding her, layer upon layer, connecting the sky to the water, the water to the land. She hears it, in every sound whispered by the elements, by the waves and the wind. It makes her soften and smile. It makes her think of sweet things.

She reaches into the black purse she has leaning against her right hip and pulls a bulgingly folded cotton towel. The old man shifts around slightly to look at her. Nadia smiles at him and sets the towel on her thighs. Then nervously, she unfolds it, exposing five cookies she presents to the comforting presence sitting by her side, "Would you like a cookie? I made them this morning."

His face brightens up, "Madame, you've read my mind. Nothing would make me happier than a freshly baked delicacy." He picks one and takes a small bite. He closes his eyes and starts chewing. His facial expression changes as if he were enjoying every texture his mouth is encountering, every flavor that is dissolving in his palate, and every ingredient that is shyly revealing itself to the probing of his inquisitive senses.

Nadia stifles a laugh, as she watches him, while blissful sensations seem to explode behind his lips, before turning to rippling waves that expand through his cheeks, and warmly flush his aged skin.

Once done chewing, he reopens his eyes and looks at her warmly, "Madame, you have my utmost respect for creating such a tasty treat." He then takes a second bite, smaller than the first, and closes his eyes, once again, to fully experience the richness of flavors melting in his mouth.

Nadia blushes, looks at the boy for a second, and then shifts her gaze to the strangely refreshing acquaintance whose path she has unexpectedly come to cross, "I don't mean to be nosy, but I'm detecting an accent in your voice, yet you speak our language perfectly… Would you mind my asking you where you're from?"

His eyes open, invitingly deep, calmingly safe, "Not at all Madame. I enjoy practicing your country's wonderful language whenever the opportunity arises." Adjusting his posture to better face her, he continues, "My people come from far away. I was born outside a Spanish village, a very short distance from the Italian borderline. My family being fairly nomadic was attached to the road and to the freedom it provides. They loved this land of yours and so every year they would cross the sea to walk on this ground, meet those who live on it, share their food, enjoy their art, observe their customs, purchase their goods, and of course be blessed by this sun."

He pauses, closing his eyes for a moment, then with a nod continues, "As the saying goes, the apple rarely falls too far from its tree. Thus, I too, following on the footsteps of my parents and grandparent, have crossed the sea to visit your land many times throughout the years. And of course, with each visit, thanks to the generosity of your country folk, I have learned a few more words."

Pleased as well as intrigued by his response, the grandmother confides, "I would have never thought that there were nomads in Spain."

"Oh, you can find nomads almost everywhere Madame," he says, with a knowing smile.

Nadia turns to check on her grandson and finds him busily collecting pebbles, amidst the boulders of his favorite playground. She looks back at the wizened man, "I really don't want to sound intrusive, and please forgive my curiosity, but when you say that you are a nomad, do you actually mean that you do not have a home?"

"Madame please, for an old man like myself, there is nothing more pleasurable than a conversation shared with a friendly and generous human being such as yourself." His eyes glisten at the sight of her cheeks turning pink. "Well… you see, as I mentioned, I was born outside a Spanish village. It had happened on the road. My parents, who were gypsies, or as some call them Roma, were refused access to the village's doctor, and no one would grant them shelter for the night. No one was willing to help. And since my mother was unable to retain me until the next village was reached, I was born in a carriage in the middle of the road, between the distantly dim lights of an inhospitable village and a guarded borderline check post, a Roma among Roma-speaking peoples. Moreover, it was on that same spot that I was named Paulo Angelo Aduro, Paulo Angelo from the Aduro tribe; and it is as an Aduro that I go through life."

Puzzled, she presses, "Forgive me but I don't understand…"

"Few are those who do, Madame, very few. My tribe is a very small one, too small to be known by others besides my own people. Years of persecution and xenophobic hatred have lowered our numbers in a dramatic way. We are an ethnicity with no land to call our own. We wander continuously, defiant of man-made boundaries, destined to remain on the road, following the wind from one place to another."

"You are just like the nomads of the desert." In her voice, he hears the vibrancy of excitement.

"Yes, indeed." He agrees, chuckling joyously.

"Don't you ever tire of not having a home where you could rest?"

"The whole world is my home, Madame."

"I'm talking about a house. You know… with walls, with a roof, and… a bed."

"That is what I mean too, Madame. The roof of my house is as high as the furthest of stars, its walls are ever so expanding, and my bed is the earth wherever my body happens to be."

"How about family?" she protests, "Those you love and care about, surely you must have a family."

He smiles again, "Of course, I do. My family is humanity as a whole, and its members are just about everywhere."

"Don't you miss anyone?" she thinks of her son, who despite being a caring and clearheaded young man, was lost to anger and despair, driven away from home to never be seen or heard from again. She remembers his warm face, his sweet smile. She remembers how much she enjoyed the sound of his clear voice. She remembers, and remembering is painful, for each memory is felt deep within. Cold grief takes hold of her heart, swallows it whole, spreading poisonous regret and pain through her veins. In anguish she aches for an answer —the right answer. A way out…

But the homeless elder remains serenely silent, observing her with compassionate eyes, his amiable lips contently closed. She tries to ask him again, but finds nothing but silence, a silence so deep it overwhelms her resolve to argue, drowns her logical-self, and leads her to disquieting nothingness, a void so large it could contain all that was lost, all that could have been, all that wasn't. She tries to look away, but grief is everywhere. It is so unavoidable it makes her want to scream and fight. But just as she's about to unleash her anger and rage, a deep sound ripples through her body. She hears, or feels cleansing vibrations she guesses to be emanating form the old man's soothing voice, penetrating into the confines of her chest cavity, speaking to, and through, her heart, pulsating in her bloodstream, vibrating in her mind, in a song she neither knows nor understands, a song she finds calming, relaxing and appeasing. Nadia sighs and lets go. She lets go of grief and pain.

Then the old traveler leans closer and says, "Let me tell you a little secret. For thousands of years our caravans have gone from village to village, from country to country, across rivers and seas, carrying in our hearts a message in which we deeply believe." His voice becomes a deep hush, a soft rippling sound as old as time itself. It melds with the world and becomes the melody of a strangely scented wind that rises and moves over the two of them.

Coming as if from nowhere, enjoyably warm, sweetly aromatic, brimming with unexpressed energy, as if carrying the taste of passion, the wind swirls around the bench, slipping along their skins, spiraling above their heads.

Then, it dies out as suddenly as it arose, leaving them, and their surroundings, impregnated in the unmistakable sweetness of cinnamon.

Paulo grins and continues, "My people found shelter beneath the branches of bountiful trees, they met beauty in the softness of flowers, they were grounded by the fertile dirt that soiled their feet, they were humbled by the miracles that come with water, they were inspired by the immensity of the sky and its countless stars, and they cried witnessing life's vibrating through, and all around, them with love and passion. And when they cried, their hearts blossomed into flowers made of light; a light of such purity and such brightness it burned through the veiling cloak of darkness and revealed Truth."

He takes another bite of the cookie, chews it slowly before swallowing it delightedly, with Nadia's eyes transfixed on his lips, "Usually, we aren't supposed to do this, but this cookie is so delicious and your company, so refreshing, I would like to share another secret with you; if you don't mind of course."

"No, no, go right ahead. You have my attention," says the old woman with a mind swirling in mystery.

Paulo gives her a conspiratorial look, "Well…" he looks around and whispers, "It's about the wind."

"The wind?" she asks with squinting eyes, gazing into his. Then, wishing to hear more, she leans toward him and whispers, "What about it?"

"It's alive. It has a mind of its own. It can hear, see, touch and even feel," Paulo nods his head slowly, as in agreement with his own statement.

The gray haired woman, confused, leans back in the silence that has sifted into the ongoing conversation, "You mean just like us?" she asks, her words inspired by a doubting thought that arises like an awakening breeze moving through the quieting fog that has somehow enveloped her mind, to question the stranger's sanity.

"No. It's beyond that, an entity unlike any other; abundant love, pure love in motion. It is everywhere, stretched over the globe, over both land and water. It reaches into the depths of our planet, and, at the same time, to its highest peaks. It knows us all, as it caresses our skins and flows within our bodies to converse with the heart and with every fiber of our beings. It hears our thoughts and sees our innermost feelings and dreams. And, as it moves from one to the other, and simultaneously through everyone, it carries bits of each and everyone, bits of everything that exists and ever existed. It moves, laden with moods and feelings, until, overwhelmed by their intensity, it becomes affected by them.

"Thus, it blows with anger through hatred, greed, envy, jealousy, selfishness, deception, for it finds them poisonously evil. And it moves gently when it finds love, passion, compassion, selflessness. For these are the qualities it is striving to collect, the qualities it is seeking to spread in their purest forms.

"This is why, my dear friend, when two hearts find one another through love, the wind is there to witness their union and bind them in passion, so that no matter what happens, no matter how far one gets from the other, they remain connected and aware of each other, ensuring that lover and beloved, mother and child, never lose one another, no matter how great the distance separating them, for the wind is always there... Yes, the wind is always there.

"That is why Madame, I never miss anyone, as long as I remember that we are so deeply connected." The strange foreigner straightens his body to face the ocean, a satisfied grin stretching his wrinkled profile.

Nadia, on the other hand, raises her eyes to the sky, her mind still holding onto the thread of his words, as they find their way into every forgotten nook and crevice within the depths of her mind and in the recesses of her heart, releasing the potency of their meaning, eating through her cloaking worries, dissolving her weighty sadness, healing her heart, appeasing her soul, until, and very suddenly, tears of joy find their way out of her reddened eyes, "Excuse me. I don't know what's taken me."

Paulo nods reassuringly, "Please Madame, there is no need for apologies."

She laughs and sniffles, "Thank you, Mister Aduro."

The old man waives his hand dismissively, "Believe me, Madame; it is I who is grateful for your generosity."

She looks at him, her eyes gleaming with intensity, perhaps revealing deeply felt emotional release.

Paulo calmly points toward the ocean, by raising his chin with a slight nod of the head, "And here comes the future."

Nadia, following his gaze, sees the little boy running toward them and starts vigorously wiping the tears that stain her face. When the boy approaches them, he slows down and begins shuffling toward his grandmother, whose flushed face is as red as a tomato. With every step taken, his eyes shift back and forth from his caring grandmother to the suspicious old man he has never seen before.

Paulo asks with a welcoming smile, "What is you name, little boy?"

The boy's eyes move indecisively from his grandmother to the stranger, seeking a clue as of what to say or what to do, until Nadia nods approvingly, "Adam, Mister."

"It is my pleasure to meet you Adam. My name is Paulo."

Adam's face, as well as posture, relaxes as he continues studying the furrowed man.

"I saw you play over there... What kind of game were you playing?"

The little boy stops next to his grandmother's legs and sets both his hands on her right knee. He lifts his heels of the ground and stretches his neck, "I'm throwing rocks in the water." His grin reveals his teeth, as he adds excitedly, "Very far in the water."

Paulo gives the jovial youngster a quizzing look and asks "You must have a strong arm."

Adam leans his torso against Nadia's kneecaps, as if to hug her shins, but instead he simply stands up again and exclaims, "I can throw very far!"

"I know. We could see you from here. And I was thinking what an interesting game it was."

Adam shrugs his shoulders relaxing to the man's presence.

"In fact, Adam, your game reminded me of one I used to play when I was your age. It was a game just like yours, but a little different."

Paulo leans toward the boy with inquisitively glowing eyes, "Would you like me to tell you about it?"

The boy nods to show his approval, then swiftly climbs on his grandmother's lap and sits facing Paulo.

"It's a game that, just like yours, requires throwing. However, I didn't throw rocks at the ocean. No, instead

I threw kisses -as many kisses as I could. I threw them in every direction and let the wind carry them to sad people, to people who have no one close by to give them a kiss and make them feel better."

"I like throwing rocks," exclaims Adam proudly.

"I have noticed." Paulo raises a hand, "but sometimes, there aren't enough or any rocks to throw."

Adjusting himself on Nadia's thighs, Adam kicks the inner sides of his feet together and smirks, "I can throw kisses too."

"I know you can," winks the old man.

The little boy hugs his grandmother, never taking his eyes from Paulo, and slowly turns his smirk to a warm smile.

"Madame, thank you for your wonderful company. It has been a pleasure talking with you. Now I have to get going." Using both his hands, Paulo pushes himself up, "I hear the wind calling."

"Would you like another cookie for the road?"

"Certainly, Madame."

"I want a cookie too," protests Adam.

Nadia laughs and hugs her little devilish treasure, "Of course you do, sweet heart."

Grabbing his backpack with both hands, Paulo sets it snuggly over his shoulders. Then, reaching for another cookie, he thanks the generous stranger for her kindness and time, and pats the boy's head, "Young man… Take care of your grandmother, will you?"

Adam grins at the old traveler who reciprocates before turning around and walking away, in the company of a lively breeze that appears to be both following and preceding him.

Skipping across an abandoned construction site, holding hands with his modestly dressed grandmother, Adam throws kisses in the air and imagines them drifting away, invisible butterflies carried by the wind, over more buildings than his eyes can see, dodging TV antennas and satellite dishes, to finally reach those who need them the most, the sad, the ill, the broken hearted, the distraught, the forgotten...

The boy raises his head to look at Nadia, feeling rather proud. She grins and ruffles his unruly soft hair with a caring hand. He returns the grin, naturally displaying the kind of unrestrained joy only someone still living in innocence is capable of experiencing. The woman's face lights up from within, as pleasant warmth filling her chest in response to the moment's sweetness. The jubilant boy hops and declares with the certainty of those who can still believe in magic, "I am making sad people smile. I'm making lonely people feel better."

Eight kilometers away, across many neighborhoods, over slowly snaking traffic lines, soot-covered buildings, decaying bureaucratic institutions, mosques, churches and synagogues, past quiet beggars and pestering street hawkers, past veiled women and burnoose wearing men, past highlighted hairdos, tightly clad skirts, high heels, Levi's Jeans, sharp-looking eye-concealing Ray Bans, cigarette smoke and cold coffee cups, past spoken Moroccan, French, Spanish and Berber, past the local and the foreign, past the hardened street thug and the corrupt law enforcement officer, past the cemetery, the overwhelmed public hospital, the school and the park, past evenly paved streets and larger than is the norm sidewalks, in a spacious pre-colonial square, a woman dressed in gray comes down the stairs of the city's court house's, an impressively large building standing at the center of the administrative quarter. Halfway down the wide staircase, she becomes aware of a soft breeze tugging at her hair, caressing her face and tickling the tip of her nose.

Usually, such experience would have irritated this attorney, driven her to stiffen in frustration and hasten her pace. On any other day, this unsolicited touch from the wind would have awakened somber thoughts, thoughts connected to bitter memories. But today, none of this happens. Today, the norm is set aside. Today, she smiles at the pleasant sensation. Today, she even ventures to entertain the image of a day that might not be as awful as she had thought.

On a clear moonlit night, while in the port of San Sebastian, Andalou found Alberto staring airily at the gray outline of his birth village, "Everything alright, old man."

"A beautiful night this is…" Alberto smiled, and then, as if to contradict his initial response, let out a sigh.

Andalou sat his arms on the ship's railing and inquired, "Do you want to go for a walk in the old neighborhood?"

Alberto gazed at the docks, "I thought about it… but, I doubt that it is a wise idea."

Andalou nodded, without uttering a word, recalling from his own experience that some pains heal better in silence.

Alberto glanced at the reserved co-worker he had become accustomed to call brother and said, "You know, I remember standing on that dock over there, with my father, on a night just like this one. I can still hear him asking me without any prelude, after reemerging from one his silent meditations, 'Alberto, did I ever tell you about the man who saved my life?' and I answered, 'No, Pa, No.' I remember him staring into the distance and saying, 'His name was Ahmed.'"

Alberto shook his head, "Ahmed. Can you believe that? So, of course, I made a remark about the name which was neither Christian nor Basque. I will never forget the way the old man pierced me with his unflinching eyes, and then said, 'That man doesn't need a Basque name to have my respect, and my gratitude. He saved my life. And for that he is my brother.' I nodded and kept my eyes down, and, believe me, had you been in my shoes, you would have done the same too.

"Anyway, and of course as you can guess, after what he had just told me, I had to find out more. So, I waited a few minutes and then began prodding about what had happened exactly. And this is, almost word for word, what my father told me on that night."

Alberto lit a cigarette and put it to his lips, "He said, 'It was December, 14, 1944. The day had just started and we were already under heavy fire from the German fortified line of defense we had been ordered to breech. Restlessness was obvious on most our faces as we waited for the order to attack and put an end to the stand-off. A second battalion -French, double our size in number, joined us. With our numbers tripled we were ready to win. When we attacked I was part of the first wave. We ran through whizzing bullets and deafening mortar shell explosions.

'I remember running downhill, through a mud field, ducking for cover in and out of craters… I was hit- three bullets, one in the right thigh, one in the left and the last between my right clavicle and shoulder. My body gave in. My riffle slipped out of my hands. I fell on my knees and then collapsed on my back. I wasn't feeling pain, but I couldn't move. It was as if I was pined to the ground. I stared at the sky, past the smoke and noise of war, and found it undisturbed, blue and calm.

'I was there for I don't know how long. It felt like an eternity. I saw a few soldiers jump over me. A boot brushed against my body. Dirt landed on my face. There was a mortar explosion near by. It shook me and left a buzzing sound in my ears. I prayed for forgiveness and waited for death. Instead, I saw a man lean down. His face was sharp and his eyes shone like dark pearls exposed to the sun. He

smiled at me and touched my shoulder. Calmly, oblivious
to the violent madness that surrounded us, he lifted his
rifle and started firing. He grabbed a grenade and lobbed
it at the Boches. He wrapped his arm around my back,
lifted me up and carried me under enemy fire, past harm's
reach and all the way to safety.

'This man I had never met before put me down, propping my back against a tree. I looked at him and saw nothing more than a blurry figure. I must have been losing too
much blood. I asked him for his name. He reached for his
water can, uncapped it and, speaking in French, asked me
to open my mouth. Mumbling, I asked him to tell me his
name. He held my head and made me drink something
that wasn't water. I tried spitting it out. But he held my
mouth shut and told me that the stuff would help until a
doctor got to me. I trusted him and swallowed his bitter
concoction. He stood up and tried to leave. But I grabbed
him from the arm, and, again, asked for his name. He
laughed and said, 'Ahmed.' I said, 'Thank you, Ahmed,'
and let go of him. He laughed and ran back toward the
enemy.

'I have no doubt that without his intervention I would
be a dead man. So a few weeks later, and right after my release from the hospital, I started looking for him. I wanted
to know why this foreign man had risked his own life to
save mine. I was, after all, a complete stranger to him. I
searched for him for months, until I ran out of leads and
out of places to search. But, this Ahmed was nowhere to
be found. It was as if the man had never existed. It was as
if he had been a mere hallucination. I tried to forget about
the whole matter. I tried, but couldn't.

'Deep inside, I knew that he was real, as real as I am.

My need to thank him made his blurry image haunt my thoughts, my dreams and nightmares. So, I continued looking for him, ignoring my own duties, responsibilities and needs. Until, one cold and damp evening, I found myself in the center of a small French village, standing alone in front of an old church whose door had been left half-opened as if for me. I walked in. The building was dark inside, except for two lit candles placed at the altar. I walked past empty pews and knelt beneath our Lord's glorious image. I stayed there for a while, maybe an hour, maybe more, praying for guidance.

'I prayed, until my mind became empty of worries. Suddenly, I felt tears running down my face. It had been ages since I could remember crying. But, I wasn't ashamed of myself, a grown man, a soldier, and all that, crying. No, I actually felt good and surprisingly at peace. It was as if a weight had been lifted from my conscience, and I could finally go on with my life. But before I could leave, I prayed for Ahmed. I called him Brother. I wished him well, and asked Our Lord to guide and protect him. When I walked out of that old church, I did so, ready to go back home, as I had finally come to terms with the possibility that I would never meet my brother again.'"

Five minutes to eight, Yasmine rings the bell of a house she used to call home. She glances at her wristwatch to make sure she is neither late nor early, before turning her eyes back on the door as it is unlocked and opened to reveal Batoul, the housemaid.

"Hello, Lalla Yasmine," Batoul, propping the door open with one hand, steps aside invitingly, "It is wonderful to see you. I have been counting the hours since Lalla announced that you were coming yesterday. Look at you! So beautiful. But, you've lost weight. Are you eating? You must be working too hard. I am so happy to see you. By the way, Lalla is waiting for you in the dinning room."

"How are you Batoul?" Yasmine smiles warmly at the woman who practically raised her, and steps in, arms extended for a hug.

Meeting her with motherly warmth, Batoul presses Yasmine against her chest, the same way she had done hundreds of times when the girl was much younger, "Very well, al-hamdoo-lil-lah. God is most generous. And how could I not be feeling well, on this glorious day. Seeing you is a blessing, Lalla Yasmine. May God almighty grant all of your wishes."

Once Batoul lets go of the girl she sincerely missed, Yasmine asks, "And your daughter, Karima, how is she?"

"She's fine. May God clear your path and hers. She passed her finals with very high scores. She also just got a job as an assistant in a pharmaceutical lab for the summer." Batoul closes the door and, raising her eyes to the heavens, exclaims, "Al-hamdoo-lil-lah! Praise to Allah, indeed!"

They start walking in through the house's garden. Yasmine puts her hand on her nanny's shoulder, "Then, next year is her last at the university. You must be very proud of her. She has been working so hard."

"Oh yes, I am very proud of her. Not a day passes without me thanking God for giving me such a wonderful daughter. Honesty and modesty. Truly, I am blessed."

"She is also very blessed for having you as a mother."

Batoul's face brightens with joy, "Thank you Lalla Yasmine. We do our best and leave the rest in His hands. Al-hamdoo-lil-lah. Al-hamdoo-lil-lah."

Yasmine smiles as she fleetingly thinks of how many times Batoul can praise Allah, and that, in the course of a single conversation, and of how she, or a younger version of her, at happier times, used to tease the caring woman who had had a lot to do with raising her for that excessive use of 'al-hamdoo-lil-lah' of hers, and then says, "Please, pass her my warmest regards and congratulate her for me." Then, seeing the barred glass door dimly lighting the end of the pathway they've taken, Yasmine slows down, "And Batoul, if she needs anything, tell her not to be a stranger, she knows where my office is."

"I will Lalla, in-cha-a-lah. I will. She'll be very de-lighted," Batoul puts her right hand on her chest, as she always does when saying in-cha-a-lah, and adds, "You are an example to her. She respects you very much." Then, reaching for the doorknob, she whispers, "Oh, by the way, Lalla Yasmine, I forgot to tell you that 'the man,' you know, is already here, inside. He arrived half an hour ago. He is... May God lead us to his light, dirty looking," she shivers, "I think he's homeless. But what do I know? ... Lalla says he's really, really good."

Yasmine rolls her eyes, "How many times did we hear her say that?"

Batoul nods in agreement, lets out a her prolonged sigh, before remembering to open the door, "Lalla Yasmine, welcome home, I am going to go ahead and get the table ready before my tongue slips and gets me in trouble."

Yasmine smiles and, swallowing her growing resentment, slowly steps into her mother's world.

Batoul follows her in, and closes the door behind them, whispering, "It is better if I stay out of it. After all, I am just a maid."

"You are more than that Batoul. You are family."

Batoul's face brightens, "God protect you, Lalla Yasmine. God protect you." Then, just as she starts walking, on her way to the kitchen, she whispers, "He's in the big room. May God protect you."

"Thank you, Batoul."

Standing in front of the large salon's double glass door, her view obstructed by hanging white embroidered curtains, Yasmine hears soft laugher coming from inside the room, the sound diluted by the austere spaciousness of the corridor. She takes a deep breath, walks in and heads for the center of a lavishly decorated room where her mother is sitting in the company of an old fellow dressed in different shades of blue. The old man sets the cup of tea he is holding on the table, stands up, and greets her.

She shakes his hand, while introductions are made, and notices that despite his poor appearance, the man speaks and carries himself with the confidence and dignity of those who never ask or expect help from others —as if he hadn't come to scheme and take, but rather to give.

A few minutes later, Batoul peaks through the opened door to announce that dinner is ready. Lalla Amina claps her hands in approval, while flourishing her well-perfected satisfied hostess smile, and invites the party to follow her to the dining room.

They cross a few hallways, leading to a couple more expensively decorated living rooms, to finally arrive in a very large dining area, where a varnished and polished long rectangular wooden table is already set. They sit in front of a dozen dishes, as many empty plates, and dazzlingly spotless crystal glasses sparkling in unison with the giant chandelier hanging above their heads. The old man nods, closes his eyes, brings his hands together and lowers his head.

He prays in silence, while Yasmine and her mother exchange surprised glances, appreciation for the pious gesture clearly showing on their faces. Lifting his head, he catches them staring at him and smiles humbly. Glancing around at the table and at her company, Lalla Amina says, "Bissmellah," three words that, in her culture, are uttered to bless the moment, as much as the action, a reminder that whatever life brings, be it abundance or penury, it is always a gift from the Sustainer, the Provider.

Then immediately after that, armed with, spoons, forks, and knifes, every one at the table begins helping themselves and eating. As dinner progresses, the hostess happily entertains her guest, whose almost magically vibrating presence feels relaxing, even to Yasmine, who can not believe how much food she's eating; but, since every dish is delicious, and since her appetite, which had been missing for some years now, seems to have returned, voracious and untamable, she doesn't try to restrain herself.

Inspired, the trio does its best to show its unquestionable appreciation for the efforts put in the creation of each dish. They praise Batoul in her absence and whenever she appears to check on them. Until having reached a point where unable to indulge anymore, they let go of the silverware, and move to a different room. On softer chairs, and around a thick wooden coffee table supported by four carved legs, each depicting a lion standing on its hind legs, they talk about life, the country and its people, about generosity and trust, about faith and love, until Batoul enters the room, pushing a double decked dessert cart, full of colorful little pastries, coffee and tea.

Setting aside all words and subjects of discussion, they make room for the talented cook with every little marvels of sweetness she has brought forth, immediately feeling pleasantly stirred by the appealing colorfulness of Batoul's culinary creations, unable to resist the pull of visual stimulation, as it prevails over other senses, and arouses their appetites once again.

Paulo stands up and reaches for the maid's hands and kisses them, making her blush and run out of the room. He says, "Thank you. Thank you," while Yasmine and Lalla Amina, tears in their eyes, lean back and surrender to laughter. They call for Batoul to come back, but to no avail. Then, they all turn to the cart and reach for what their eyes desire. They bite and forget about time.

Paulo helps himself with another cup of tea and asks Yasmine if she wouldn't mind accompanying him on a walk around their beautiful garden, for it seems very large and he doesn't want to get lost in it. The mother frowns realizing that she isn't invited, but refrains from objecting. Yasmine agrees, pours herself a cup of black coffee, and invites him to follow her.

As Yasmine and Paulo step outside, their senses are immediately touched and awakened by a coolly refreshing breeze that remains with them as they start walking along the garden's dimly lit pathway.

Paulo ambling alongside Yasmine, looking admiringly around him, begins, "It is such an extraordinary place. It must take your mother a lot of effort to keep it this way."

"She enjoys taking care of her plants. It is probably the only activity she appreciates partaking in, and even more so since father passed away." Yasmine hears resentment in her voice, and tries to hide it in a smile.

But Paulo, still looking absorbed by the enchanting grounds surrounding them, doesn't seem to be paying attention to her. Yet, when he speaks, to Yasmine, it sounds as if every word has thoroughly been considered, "She is a very strong woman, and she cares about you a great deal."

The frustrated daughter replies, "More than she needs to, if you ask me."

The old man nods, "I am sure she just wants the best for you."

"For me?" she protests, "Sometimes I wonder if it isn't more for her own wellbeing that she does what she does."

"She is a mother…" Paulo stops and looks up, as if at Creation's infinity.

Yasmine sighs, "So, what is it that you do anyway?"

He smiles, "I'm trying to find stars."

She raises her eyes to the sky, and smirks, "No, I mean… what kind of healer are you?"

He lowers his gaze to meet hers, "I'm no healer. I'm just a simple traveler."

Yasmine stares at him, perplexed, and clearly interested by his ambiguous reply. "If you're no healer, why am I here then?"

Paulo tilts his head slightly, "I don't know about you, all I know is that I came here to eat."

She smiles, feeling better about being where she is, no longer regretting having shown up, and lets out a playful frown, "You realize that this doesn't make any sense."

Pensively, he rubs his stubbly chin using his thumb and index fingers, "Not really." He straightens his head and takes a small sip of tea, "I think that it is always good to pay a visit to those we love and care for, and that it never hurts to meet new faces... Aren't we, after all, social creatures?"

She looks at him askance, "...you mean to tell me that you aren't here because of my condition.'

His eyebrows curl up questioningly, deepening many lines on his forehead, "Condition? What condition, if you don't mind my asking?"

She sighs, "I really hope you aren't leading me on, Mister Aduro."

He raises his right hand, "I give you my word of honor that I'm not 'leading you on.'"

Yasmine, hesitant, glances behind her, to the house, and then back at Paulo, "I am totally confused. I thought that you were another traditional healer my mother hired to fix what modern medicine has failed to amend."

"And, what exactly are we talking about here?"

"I can't get pregnant," she shrugs her shoulders, adding, "and my mother believes that someone placed a curse on me." She shakes her head, before glancing resentfully over her shoulder, and says, "There is no word to describe how pushy she can be." Then, turning to face the old man, finds signs of understanding and support in the way he is looking at her, and decides to speak her mind, "God! She has been dragging me from one charlatan to another for two years now."

Paulo nods, "I see, and I am deeply sorry for you."

Yasmine frowns, "Are you sure you're not here because of that?"

Sounding almost amused, the guest replies, "My dear, what can I possibly do about such an affliction. I am neither a doctor, nor a healer. I am just an old traveler who was invited to share a meal and a conversation."

"Oh…" Yasmine softens, ready to believe the truth he is sharing, and ignore those he is concealing.

"If I may ask," his eyes squint, "How is your husband taking it?"

Yasmine lowers her head and stares into the somber and neatly mowed grass stretching in front of her feet, as her mind drifts into a subject she'd rather leave behind, and finally answers, "I'd rather not talk about that…"

"Of course. Of course." Paulo sighs, "You know my dear, holding such things inside for too long can be very hurtful. Sometimes, opening up to someone else can be relieving." He pauses to smile at her as she lifts her head, "Plus, I am just a wandering old man. It's very improbable that you will ever see me again," and raising his hands, palms facing the sky, "Think about it, talking to me is like talking to the wind. None of those you know will ever find out anything about what is being said, here tonight, between the two of us."

Yasmine takes a deep breath and invites him to continue their walk. He offers her his arm and she takes it. "Mister Aduro you are a very odd man. And for some reason, I feel very comfortable around you." Then, as they pass under a branch that hangs arched above the pathway, she reaches up and gently touches the leaf closest to her head. "My marriage is a mess," sadness distorts her voice, "I married someone I have absolutely no feelings for," she sets her eyes on the ground ahead of them, "absolutely none," and bites her lower lip, as if guiltily. "On the other hand," she laughs bitterly, "He hates me. He's hated me ever since we found out I am incapable of giving him offsprings."

She stops, as a few strands of hair, annoying escapees from the grip of the rubber band used to keep her face clear, dangling teasingly, touch her cheek. Quickly, she brushes them back and behind the ears.

Paulo smiles, having caught a glimpse of someone else, someone she used to be, a happier and freer version of the restrained soul standing next to him, "Did you ever think about adopting?"

"Adopting!" She repeats bitterly, "I suggested adoption! And my husband, if I can still call him that, got really upset. He told me that it was out of the question. He wants children of his own —his own kin and blood, and nothing less."

Paulo sighs. He allows silence to set in, so that she may fill it with words of which she so direly needs to let go. He waits quietly, giving her time and attention, because he has learned a very long time ago that sometimes what people need the most is to be listened to and acknowledged. He stays close to her, his heart open, without any reservations or expectations, until what ought to be relinquished is ready to come out.

Surely enough, in due time, Yasmine begins pouring her heart out, telling him about her nights, the emptiness she feels in the mornings, her husband's love for another woman, and that fear that keeps them both from doing anything that would allow them to escape their binding misery. It all comes out rushing out of her mouth so fast she can't believe having said any of it.

"Some things aren't meant to be, just as some couples aren't meant for one another," as Paulo speaks, Yasmine feels caught in a warm breeze unlike any she'd ever felt before, "Denial is never the answer," she wonders if her imagination is playing tricks on her, or if she is really effortlessly moving, carried by an invisible river, a river made of wind, "Whatever is founded on a mistake, or based on a lie, is bound to failure, no matter how much stitching is applied."

They stop, surrounded by roses and thorns, breathe in air that embraces them richly scented with a fragrance deeply bound to, and reminiscent of, pleasures from yesteryears.

Paulo continues, "And going ahead while ignoring what is broken can only lead to pain, sadness, and eventually disaster." He looks deeply into her eyes as she listens, "Life demands from us to be true to ourselves, to stop forging ahead, to retrace our steps to the point where we began seeing our lot as dark and awful instead of bright and wonderful, a point where love changed to hatred, and then, when we get to that point, it is there that we have to make the change, to find closure and be able to start over with a clean slate."

Yasmine murmurs, "You think it's that simple?"

"I understand that it's hard, especially when it wasn't your fault, when those who love you went ahead, with the best of intentions, and intervened destroying what was pure and, consequently, broke your heart, that loving heart of yours, so loving and so opened." His eyes, like wells of tenderness, welcome her, as she runs his words through her head a second time.

"What are you talking about?"

Calmly, he answers, "I don't need to name names, do I? You know very well that which I am talking about. You're a bright woman, an attorney used to analyzing words, used to extracting valuable meaning out of what could be lies, and what could be truth."

She flares her nostrils and breathes out like a challenged warrior, in reaction to feeling swallowed by the depth of his irises, before looking away, "This is all nonsense…"

"It is your eyes, my child. Your eyes could never lie, and they're speaking loudly for you. Your eyes are filled with hatred, a hatred that once was love."

Suddenly, Yasmine feels an emotional flood bursting through her as his words reach her mind, as if to dissolve inside her head, turn to a warm emotional elixir meant to sluice down and around every single defense she's erected within, and to finally reach her heart –her broken heart– in a stirring and intoxication trickle.

"Your heart has once known love in its purest form. I can tell… Its dying flame still shows through your eyes." Speaking softly, he offers soothing benevolence in the tone of his voice, "Why hate Yasmine, why?"

"He abandoned me." The answer escapes as a murmur

that surprises Yasmine, as it lingers, as if caught by the breeze.

"Perhaps, he was as much of a victim as you were. Perhaps, the choice wasn't really his. And perhaps, his betrayal was an act of self-sacrifice inspired by his love for you, by hopes of wonderful days to come. If this was the case Yasmine, if this was how it really happened, I ask you Yasmine, would it be right for you to hate him?"

Yasmine extracts herself from Paulo's penetrating gaze and starts walking away, but only to take a few steps, stop, turn around and shout angrily in his direction, "Why are you defending him? He broke my heart!"

Paulo Aduro doesn't react. He simply stands still, calmly, unmoved by her anger, "Ignoring the problem will only allow it to grow until you can no longer pretend that it doesn't exist, but then, it will be too late. Or, is it already too late? I can tell that it isn't, can you? There is still a chance for peace and happiness -if you want..."

Yasmine sees him draw in closer, yet she is sure he isn't walking or moving at all, "You have already waited too long." His voice fills her mind, "I know that you care about the ones around you. Why then, allow this problem to hurt them through you? Wouldn't it be better to just put an end to all of it? Answer me, Yasmine?"

Yasmine cries, "I can't, you don't understand... I can't."

"No, you can... We both know that you can, Yasmine." He insists, "Listen to your heart. It is aching for a new beginning, a new chapter. It is aching for deliverance and peace."

Melting within, losing all of her defenses, those she built herself and those erected by other, standing naked at truth's door, vulnerable to the winds of awakening, Yasmine says, "I don't know how to do it…"

"There is nothing to it. Just listen to your heart, it will lead you." His smile blossoms as he whispers, "Just listen, the same way I do." He brings his right hand to his chest, "Do you known what my heart tells me?" He reaches for her right hand and puts it where his was, "Listen. Do you feel my heartbeat?"

Yasmine nods and replies shyly, "Yes, but…"

"If you listen carefully, it will tell you a lot about me. It will tell you how I enjoy watching the sky, the brilliance of old stars, the sounds of nature, the sweetness of life, as well as the bitterness left at the wake of fleeting time. It will tell you what wonders I feel in the very breath that flows through me, as well as through everyone else. It will tell you about the taste of true ecstasy. It will tell you about the sighting of true love's irresistibly consuming flames, which no matter how faint they are, can never be denied.

"Yasmine, Listen. Feel. See. They're there, warm and lively flames, perhaps just like the one burning in your eyes and in your heart, that beautiful heart of yours, which has so much to say, which begs you to listen as it tells you what you have to do."

Releasing her hand, he watches her withdraw it silently, "No amulet, no potion, no doctor will be able to help you with this. Yet, the solution is much simpler than you ever thought. You might even have known it all along. Just give yourself some time and listen to your heart."

They reach a sleeping rose on the edge of the pathway. Paulo caresses it softly and closes his eyes.

Yasmine follows his chapped fingers as they brush,

ever so lightly, against the flower's glistening beauty, and says, "I'm tired."

The old man replies, his eyes still on the peacefully resting rose, "I know you are."

Yasmine gazes at the crimson rose, so fragile and trusting in contrast with the hard and callused, but nonetheless caring hand, and sees herself, fragile and lost, ready to trust, but afraid to believe only to be hurt. And seeing, she asks, "Will you help me?"

"I am just an old passerby, who sometimes shares what little wisdom I carry around. I told you what I see. The rest is up to you." Then, he smiles and looks up at the sky.

She follows his gaze, and finds eternity. Suddenly reality is altered, and Yasmine feels like falling into the night's void, disoriented as if succumbing to vertigo, until Paulo pulls her back.

"Let me tell you about a village in Spain, somewhere in Andalusia. It is a small fishing village with a beach where rest a little more than a dozen wooden fishing boats, surrounded by hundreds of seagulls nestled in the sand, between the sea and a wall, a wall that has become quite an attraction these last couple of years."

Ignoring the look of shock on Yasmine's face, he continues, "On the wall is a painting called 'Esperanza.' And if I recall correctly, the painting depicts a woman of great beauty and serene disposition, whose sight is said to be capable of restoring hope in those who lost it, capable of healing hearts that were broken."

He pauses, rubbing his forehead, and then proceeding mundanely, "From what I've heard, this Esperanza, and ever since it was painted, has been attracting a great deal of visitors. People with broken hearts and lost hopes, from all parts of the world, have been stopping at that beach to stand in front of the mural, in order to cry, heal, and find closure. Now, I don't know how true this story is, but you should look into it. It might be helpful. The world is full of miraculous gifts. And if you can believe, everything is possible."

Yasmine remains speechless, baffled by the fact that the beach Paulo described is the exact background of that recurring dream that has been haunting her nights, with that child staring at her with tears in his eyes, the silhouette of a man hidden in a cloak of shadows, and her, frozen with fear, unable to move, as if she were paralyzed.

Bewildered, lost with hundreds of questions clamoring for her attention, speechless with too many words knotted in her throat, she can only stare blankly at the old man who somehow, and in the most leisurely of ways, mentions the affliction that has been pulling her out of sleep in the middle of the night and causing her to lie awake in the dark.

"Are you alright my child?" Paulo stares at her worriedly.

"Yes, I think so." She pauses hesitantly, "Would you mind if we went back inside. I am getting cold."

"Of course not, my dear. Of course not."

They head back to the house, following blurry spheres of lights which, emanating from equally-spaced lampposts, dimly illuminate the graveled winding path that ends and begins at the doorsteps of the house.

Yasmine stops at the door and, clearing her throat, looks at Paulo, "Out of curiosity Mister Aduro, do you know the name of the village you were telling me about?"

Paulo shakes his head, "No, my dear. All I know is the name of the painting. The village is very small, you see... very few people had heard about it before that mural was painted. But, what I know for sure is, if the story has any truth in it, it is on the coast of the province of Andalusia."

He opens the door and holds it for her. As she passes him and enters the house, he closes his eyes, allowing, for a second, a satisfied smile to light his features.

"Do you think that she'll be alright?"

Paulo looks at Amina, "There is always hope."

"I worry so much about her."

Paulo nods, "Guilt is a heavy burden to carry."

Lalla Amina shakes her head, "It's not her fault if she can't give him a child."

"I'm not talking about Yasmine."

"I'm not following you, Senor Paulo…"

"I suggest you look within. Look within and face the guilt you're tired of carrying. How long has it been? How long have you been living with so much shame? How long has it been since you stood in love's path? How long has it been since your good intentions turned sour?"

"Good inten… Oh, my god!" Taken aback, her eyes widen. She puts her right hand over her opened mouth, looks away, and asks, her voice afflicted with disarray, "Does Yasmine know? She must… How else would you know?"

"Yasmine doesn't know. But, your heart does. And whatever is in the heart, the eyes cannot hide."

Nostrils flared, hands shaking, she gazes away and then back at Paulo, "You don't understand…"

The old man interrupts, "Your daughter is in pain. What else do I need to understand?"

Lalla Amina stands up, her face distorted in panic, and shouts, "How dare you judge me? How dare you blame me?"

He presses himself onto his feet, and answers quietly, "I'm not the one who's judging and blaming. Guilt is usually a personal issue, even if at times it doesn't appear so."

"Get out of my house." she yells.

Paulo sighs and walks away, "It's never too late to undo what was unjustly done."

"Oh! The nerve! Get out!" she commands, unable to hold herself from shaking.

"There is only one way to peace, Madame." He opens the living room's glass door, steps out, and closes it behind him.

Left alone, Lalla Amina collapses on the closest sofa and, burying her face in her palms, begins sobbing, succumbing to the pain of past deeds. Curling into sadness, feeling cornered, she suffers, as guilt, unearthed and awakened, goes on stabbing at her heart again and again, showing no mercy, allowing no respite.

It had been four years since a figure clad in black entered the small fishing village. He appeared, carrying a large sailor bag slung over his left shoulder, wearing a pair of black jeans, army boots and a black pea coat. He was walking with a straight gait, despite the sadness adorned by his face.

He stopped at Maria Santiago's door, knocked and waited, never taking his right hand from his coat pocket. Many villagers, gathered along the wall of a nearby home, were watching him suspiciously; he was a stranger in a place outsiders usually left alone. He ignored them, deeply absorbed by a letter he carried in that pocket, sealed in an envelope he could neither forget, nor stop touching with the fingers of his right hand.

Hearing the sound of foot steps behind the door, he took a deep breath to alleviate the feeling of tightness felt in his chest. The door handle turned with a squeak, and a woman whom he recognized as Maria appeared holding a kitchen towel in one hand. She was much older than the only picture he had seen of her, an old photograph of a young woman shyly smiling at the camera.

She looked at him questioningly, "Yes, How may I help you?"

Uneasy, he shifted on his feet, "Maria Santiago?"

"Yes…" she spoke anxiously.

He coughed, and stammering began, "I… have a… a… mmmh… a letter for you. It's from your –your, your husband Al-Alberto." He pulled the envelope out of his pocket.

Pallor spread through her face, her hand frightfully tightened its grip on the towel she had been holding, "Where is Alberto? Did something happen to him?" Her eyes bulgingly opened, as she held her breath unable to resist succumbing to the panic that was quickly taking hold of her.

The stranger looked at the crowd that was gathering behind him, "May I come in? Please…"

Shaking, she wavered, before wearily stepping aside to allow him in. He walked in followed by the sound of her breath getting louder and faster, and almost went numb when her voice, soaked in liquid fear, hit him as she cried in shear desperation, "Where is Alberto?"

He turned to face her. But, as soon as his eyes met hers, he lowered his gaze, "I am afraid that Alberto…" He could not finish the dreaded sentence.

She let go of the towel, and uttered a weak objection, "No…" She raised her hand toward him, "No!" She fell to her knees, holding her face in her hands, and broke down crying convulsively.

Overwhelmed, the stranger found himself incapable of moving. He waited for what seemed to be an eternity. He waited until the widow had no more tears to shed, until she became too weak to go on wailing, and until he could think clearly again about what he would have to tell her next. He helped her onto her feet and led her to the kitchen which he could see through an opened door. He sat her on a chipped wooden chair, and began rummaging around, opening and closing cabinets, until he found what a glass he could fill with water.

He gave her the glass and helped her take a sip, and another. Too exhausted to argue, she drank, then, staring blankly at the cup she was holding in her hands, thanked him.

He nodded and looked at the envelope he was still holding in his hand, "Would you like to read the letter?"

Struggling to talk, she managed to ask, "What does it ...say?"

"I don't know. I didn't open it." He felt sorry for not having a better answer.

After wiping her reddened eyes and chafed nose, she grabbed the envelope shakily, and began examining it, slowly, from every possible angle, as if searching for some clue that would tell her what lay hidden inside. She then looked up at the man who was standing in her kitchen, a stranger she had never met, but whom she could nevertheless name, and asked, "How long have you known Alberto?"

"Three or four years... We've shared bunks, for at least two of them." He looked at the floor, "He was like a father to me."

She waited for him to look at her again before asking, "Do you know how he died?" Her face, emotionally devastated beyond words, begged for an answer.

The man lowered his eyes again, and tried to explain, his voice heavy with sadness, "He... fell overboard during a violent storm."

Maria took a constrained breath, "When did it happen?"

"Eight days ago." He had been counting the days, living them in the company of loss and pain.

"Do you think he suffered?" Her hand clung desperately onto the black blouse she was wearing.

"No, he didn't. Everything happened very quickly," he paused, his eyes brimming with tears, "We were both there, pulling the net out of the water, when a wave crashed over us..."

He shook his head and looked away, "We were swept over the deck. I slammed against the railing. I saw him hit the water and disappear... I'm sorry." Then, and as if the sound of his own voice was becoming too much of a burden, he sat down, "I tried... fastened a rope to my waist and dove after him," he gazed at the floor, surrendering to blame and regret, "I'm so sorry... it was too dark and the water was too cold."

"So... there is no body?" She started crying again.

"No, Senora," he sounded apologetic, "All I have is a letter and a few of his belongings."

She wiped the tears that wouldn't stop falling, looked at him, and asked, already knowing the answer to her question, "What is your name?"

"Andalou."

Maria nodded and shifted her gaze to the envelope. She took a deep breath and opened it very carefully. Andalou watched her silently, as she pulled a white paper, unfolded it, and began reading in silence, sobbing and sniffling.

Maria, my love,

As I am about to write this letter, I find my mind filled with memories of you and I, memories of us holding Caesar. I find myself missing you and thinking how I wish you and little Caesar were by my side-- how I wish I were home instead of being so far away in the middle of this cold sea. Then, I remember that this is the way it has to be... Life has given us so very little choice, besides struggle... So very little choice, even now, that too many years have passed, that my body is weakening, helplessly decaying, and that in my heart has germinated the heavy feeling that my time has come. I hope that it is simply my imagination playing tricks on me, however, and just in case, what I am feeling is right, meaning that we will not be seeing each other again —at least in this life, I decided to write you this dreadful letter. And trust me when I say that even as I cannot help feeling this fatalistic about what is to come, I am hoping and praying that I will make it back home and that you will not have to read the sad words of a tired man, for I can only imagine how hard it would be. However, my sweet Maria, if it isn't written that I should return, I pray that you will forgive me for whatever sorrow this letter might bring to you. I pray that I won't have caused you too much pain, and that you will not cry too much, since just like me, you can see that as I leave, I do so with much happiness in my heart. I feel the warmth of our love, and I am sure that it will be there all the way to the end. I know that I will smile when all the lights go out. My dearest Maria, you and I have gone through so much. From the first time you touched my face and received my heart to the last time I waved you good-bye. Our memories together, as long as I live, are more precious to me than the breath that keeps me alive. Nothing could compare to the true love we share. That is why Maria, I don't want you to be sad. I don't know what comes after death, yet I am ready for whatever it is, because I am certain that if there is a way for us to be together again, we will. But until then Maria, I want you to tell Caesar that I love him, teach him how to be honest and dignified. Maria, sweet and lovely Maria, I want you to stop worrying, to take care of yourself and to enjoy life's blessings. I want you to laugh, and drink to life, to beauty and to love. As for the man who handed you the letter, he has made me a promise, and if he is still there as you are reading these lines, he is indeed keeping it. You can call him Andalou. He is like the brother I once had and lost. He is the one I have been writing about every now and then, for the last three years. For some reason, I have come to trust him more than myself, perhaps because he has saved my life twice already. Anyway, because of the things that have been going through my mind lately, I have asked him to promise me that if I were to die on this journey, he would look after you and Caesar, and that he would never set foot on a ship again. In exchange, I am giving him half of that stretch of land I bought and never used. The other half is yours to do with as you please. I have asked him to be there for you when you need help. I have taught him most of what I know so that he would pass it on to Caesar —I hope that you understand. On the land I give him, I asked him to erect a building with a wall facing the sea. On that wall -I made him swear- that he will paint something representing hope and reconcilia-tion. Let the rest of the village know about my decision.

And please, treat him as if he really were my brother, and trust, as I do, that I leave you in good hands, my lovely and precious Maria.

Maria, I hope and pray that we will meet again.

Yours forever,

Alberto Santiago Vantisso

Struggling to breathe, Maria looked at Andalou, tears flooding her eyes, and managed to say, "Welcome home, Andalou."

Later on that day, and not too long after sunset, a meeting took place, inside Maria's house. Twenty five people, all neighbors, gathered tightly in the widow's living room and stared, reservedly at Andalou, while listening to their host as she shared the details of her late husband's wishes. Once she was done, and nothing was left for her to say, five elders retreated to the kitchen to drink wine and discuss what they had heard and what the village should do.

Behind a closed door, they consulted with one another for over an hour, and finally reappeared to let everyone know that they had decided to respect Alberto's desires. Alberto had left them no choice. He was dead, and the dead was better left unchallenged. There were too many stories out there about spirits haunting and tormenting the unwise living.

Thus, it was for the best of everyone involved that they agreed to respect the dead man's wishes. One after the other, they hugged and welcomed Andalou. Then, as the occasion was as good as any other, they had a toast in his honor. A short and stocky man sang some old local song, accompanied by a toothless musician playing on the strings of a time seasoned guitar. It was a song about mourning and loss. It was a song about stolen goodbyes and gray days.

After the villagers left the house that night, Maria and Andalou found themselves, shrouded in thick silence, one grieving her loss and wondering what life had brought to her doorstep, the other trying to accept the improbability of his fate, both hoping they will be able to make the best out of what life had handed them.

Maria felt tired and heartbroken. She had gone through a great deal of suffering, and was expecting more of the same. Life had been harsh, unfair. Yet, it was clear to her that she could not give up. She was a mother and a fighter. She had already gone through hell. 'Why not keep on going?' she argued. She owed it to herself, and if not to herself, then to the boy.

Andalou felt tired and lost. He was tired of running, tired of fighting. He was tired of a life that barely gave and always took. Yet, he would not surrender. He had gone through hell. But no, he couldn't give up. He would go on, he owed it to himself, and if not to himself then definitely to Santiago, the Spanish sailor in whom he had found a brother, as well as a mentor. He would fulfill his part of the bargain. He would keep the promise he had made to the teacher who taught him the art of carpentry and opened his eyes to the beauty of raw wood and the endlessness of possibilities it offers.

The more he thought of it, the more Andalou could see that he had no other choice. His world was unforgiving. A promise was a promise, was a promise. For the given word was as heavy as any action taken, as any deed performed. He had learned that the hard way. He had paid dearly. He had hit rock bottom. He had fallen into the pit of darkness and despair. Then, and for reasons that are completely beyond him, he was given a second chance. A door opened. A path was revealed. The past was the past was the past. The present became nothing but an action, free of speculation, free of doubt. The future seized to exist.

Andalou would act. He would neither compromise, nor second guess in the name of tomorrow. He would not disappoint the friend who had introduced him to the freedom found on the tip of a paint brush as it touches an inviting white canvas. He would struggle and strive to honor the memory of the guiding soul that led him to the magic revealed at the cutting edge of a chisel as it runs through the formless. He would persevere for the one who taught him how to use his hands as a means to channel and release the very feelings he carried within, trapped in his heart. Yes, He would stand unwavering in the face of the unknown for the crazy man who sent him to this forgotten village so that he may inherit a widow, a child he hadn't met yet, a shop he still had to build and a wall he still had to paint.

Just Yesterday, Isaam Jazil unlocked the door of his apartment, sat the brown lather briefcase he owned for more than twenty years on the old hickory table standing against the hallway's wall, and shouted his wife's name three times, "Nadia. Nadia. Nadia."

"Would you stop shouting like a mad man already? I'm in the kitchen," came her reply, followed by, "What's wrong?"

Isaam rushed through the hallway, a small central living room and toward his wife's voice, "You won't believe what happened to me…"

Not used to seeing her husband this excited, Nadia sat down the knife she was using to peel a plateful of uncooked yellow potatoes and stood up and away from the cooking table to greet her life companion, "What? What happened? Are you alright?"

He reached for her hands, brought them to his lips, kissed them and said, with a voice full of urgency, "Sit down, so I can tell you."

She took a deep breath, let him lead her back to the chair he found her sitting on, before speaking her mind, "In the name of God, speak already. You're making me nervous."

Smiling like a child who was had just made a grand scale discovery, he pulled a chair from underneath the table and sat in front of his attentive wife. He took a deep breath and began, in a hushed tone Nadia thought more appropriate for the revealing of juicy secrets, "Less than an hour ago, I was sitting at the café, with the old gang, when, all of a sudden, I heard this whistling…"

Isaam stopped talking, interrupted by Nadia who put

her right palm against his forehead, and asked, "What are you doing?"

Nadia raised an eyebrow and, sounding like a worried mother, answered his question with her own, "You feel warm... Are you sure you're alright?"

Isaam smirked and frowned, deeming both expressions as the best possible response to Nadia's questions, then and because he loved his life's partner with the passion of a thousand inspired poets, he smiled tenderly and responded, "I'm fine, believe me, just let me finish, will you?"

Nadia sighed, because dinner still needed to be attended to, and who could tell how long this story of his was going to take to be told, explained and discussed, but seeing how intense the man was, she acquiesced and let him share.

"So, like I was saying, I heard this whistling, and I couldn't believe my ears, because the whistling was a tune from my village. In fact it was the tune of a song composed by some inspired Bedouin from my tribe. Do you hear that? The tune played was that of my tribe's song, an old song I haven't heard since my father died... Can you believe that?" He stared at his wife, astonishment readily visible on his face.

"And that's what you're so excited about, someone whistling the tune of an old pastoral song?" Nadia asked, sounding rather unimpressed, "Have you lost your mind?"

Isaam dismissed the question with a wave of his hand, "Nadia, my gentle dove, I know this might sound silly, but try to understand. I haven't heard this song from anyone else but my father... and I distinctly remember asking him about it once, only to be told that his father had thought him the song before disappearing during the war. I mean, who would know it, even I had forgotten about it. So for a second, I imagined I would see a relative walking past the cafe, a cousin, although most of them are dead. But then, I spotted the whistler, an old and poor looking fellow, more wrinkled than the whole troupe I was sitting with. And guess what, he looked at me and smiled… as if he knew who I was, as if he knew what his whistling meant for me.

Nadia held her breath, suddenly recalling the old man she had met by the lighthouse, earlier that day when she was spending time with her grandson. She straightened her back, and quickly asked, "So? What did you do?"

"I ran out to catch the old man before he disappeared, and when I did, I asked him where he'd learned that melody, and told him about my father and bout the song's origins."

"And what did he say?" as she posed her question, her attention was already hanging is suspension waiting for the answer that would come out of his lips and to the meaning they might carry within.

"Well, he told me that he had learned it from a friend of his, someone he had traveled with by foot across Spain, more than thirty years ago," Isaam was so excited that as he spoke he failed to notice the new intensity that had appeared in Nadia's gaze.

Nadia opened her mouth to mention Paulo Aduro, certain that she and her husband had both met with the same man, but couldn't place a single word.

Isaam, too involved in sharing what had happened to him, was unable to give her a chance to speak, "Hearing that old man, a foreigner I could tell from his accent, talk, I became even more interested in him, so I invited him to join me at the café in order to talk a bit longer, because, somehow, I felt the need to find out more."

He took a deep breath, "I led him to my table, and to the group, and somehow, as soon as they saw him, they stopped arguing, which was utterly unprecedented. I could not believe my eyes, and I began wondering what sort of man it was I had accosted. It was as if he had brought peace along with him, and the breeze, let me tell you this, if I didn't know any better, I would swear that it had been following him around, and when he sat, it died out all of the sudden, as if he and the wind were one and the same."

"The wind was following him," Nadia spoke softly.

"Just about," leaning closer to Nadia, he looked into the beautiful brown eyes that had known him through life's hardships and pleasures, and added in the most conspiratorial of tones, "Being around this man was an experience that defied logic, from beginning to end. I have never seen, or been through, anything of the sort. When he started talking, his voice overtook me. It drowned out every other sound and noise. I could swear it was calling for my attention. And it wasn't just me who felt that way, no the others too, they seemed mesmerized by his words, staring the way they did, like children captivated by a great story-teller, their mouths half opened, their eyes wide and unblinking, and their attention completely drawn to a single point –the foreigner."

"Isaam…" Nadia tried to speak, but her husband raised both hands. He seemed about ready to leap from his chair.

"Just let me finish, please, let me share with you what this strange fellow told me about the friend he had learned the song from, for he sang it too, as he knew its verses by heart. Listen to this. He said that he had been taught that song by a man he had met whilst traveling from northern Spain and heading south toward the Mediterranean. When I asked him to tell us more about that man, He explained that his friend was from the Riff region. He had left his country seeking revenge from Franco and his government, had fought many a battle, living like a beast in the Iberian wilderness, and moving like a shadow in the night, until his enemy's death brought an end to his quest. Then, this man from the mountains threw away his riffle and began heading south.

"He said that was when they met, on a road, tired and famished, but too proud to show it. And from there, they walked together, for days and days, weeks and weeks, until the Sea appeared to them, blue and vast, its breath like a hushing song, peaceful and appeasing. They had reached a deserted beach, when the old man from the Riff, fell to his knees on the wet sand and wept. He wept, the foreigner said, his grief, his loss, his past, until there were no tears left in him to give. Then he sat still and stared at the sea, or perhaps beyond it, where his family had once been, and where his heart will always dwell. Later that day, that man told this very foreigner who suddenly appeared in my life that he could not go any further, that he would stay there, for he had come as close as he could to his sorrow.

"And as I heard that, Nadia, I knew, without a shadow of a doubt, that the man this strange foreigner was speaking of was my grandfather. Yes, the grandfather who left his country to pursue his enemy and never came back, the grandfather who was consumed by pain and a need to seek revenge. Yes. The man from the Riff was my grand father…"

Isaam shook his head, as if taken aback by his own narrative, "So, I asked him if he'd seen his friend again. And guess what? He had. He said that his friend had remained on that beach, right next to a small village that soon adopted him as one of their own. They gave him some land where he built himself a comfortable home and where he spent the rest of his days, a fisherman among other. He died peacefully and surrounded by friends who comforted him until the very end…"

Isaam stopped talking, as he became aware of the tears that were filling his eyes to the brim. He chuckled, moved as sadness and happiness chased each other inside his chest.

Nadia stroke his face with her comforting hands, "Oh, my dear."

He gazed at her and found that she too was crying. He pulled his chair closer to hers, and kissed her forehead with utmost tenderness. Then, tenderly stroking her hair, he asked, "Why the tears, my dear?"

She laughed and sniffled, "You won't believe what happened to me today…"

Isaam gave her a puzzled look, "What happened? Tell me. Surely it cannot be any stranger than what I shared with you…"

Nadia sighed, not knowing how to explain the unexplainable, or how to make words convey the depth of the feelings she had found in a stranger's company. Yet, and after taking a deep breath, she began sharing her story, revealing her encounter with a man named Paulo Aduro, yes Paulo Aduro, the same man her husband had just been talking about, and by the time she was finished Isaam was left at loss for words.

Isaam shook his head and hugged the caring and tender companion whom he could never live without. She hugged him back and rested her head against his, for it was his shoulder she had learnt to lean against in the hardest times. They found each other, as they had done throughout the years, two loving souls tending to each others' wounded hearts. Thus, they remained, sustained by their closeness, their hearts beating in unison, feeling blessed, as they accepted life's gift, no matter how strange and mysterious it might seem, as what had transpired could not be explained, but was undoubtedly felt and that surely was enough.

Running through a dark forest of trees with over-reaching branches, Yasmine is too terrified to look back. She's been running forever, lost in a frightening forest she cannot escape. Suddenly, she stumbles upon a pathway and follows it. Rushing through darkness, aware that the forest is behind her, screeching and wailing, an evil song that chills her to the bone, she sees a dark tower at the end of the pathway.

She sprints towards this eerily standing structure, desperation overwhelming all her senses, not knowing what is awaiting her. With the disquieting sensation that it is the tower that is coming to meet her, she makes her way along the edge of a cliff, against which she can hear the ocean's waves violently crushing.

She enters the tower, swallowed by its expanding entrance, and finds herself in the darkness of her childhood home. She climbs upstairs. The walls sway in and out like blurred shadows dancing in drunkenness. The stairs are wet and slippery, glistening along with the flickering light of a swinging chandelier.

Stepping into a corridor of thick penumbra, she searches blindly for light switch, but has to give up, as she is swallowed by a thick veil of pure darkness that releases her in front of a door behind which she knows there is light. She pushes the door open and finds herself facing the room she had grown in.

Wearily, she enters the old and familiar space and discovers that she isn't alone. There is someone sitting on her bed. She wants to turn around and run away, but instead she walks toward the bed. The large silhouette is facing the other way. She walks around the bed, but the face spins away from her. She walks faster, but to no avail. She stops and screams helplessly. The silhouette turns around and faces her.

Yasmine, breathless, speechless, backs away, until she is stopped by the wall.

Her mother shrouded in black, holding what could only be a severed heart in her hands, gives a beastly snarl. Hissing, She bites into the heart, without taking her eyes from her daughter. Yasmine presses her back against the wall, unable to move. Amina's mouth is oozing blood. She begins laughing, and her laughter is painfully cold. In her eyes there is nothing but evil.

Yasmine collapses, panting and gasping for air. She wants to get up and run away, but her legs refuse to respond to her pleas. She is shattered. She is broken. She is so small and her mother is a giant beast. She looks away and down, and finds a motionless body lying on the floor, in a pool of dark blood. The cadaver is close enough for her to touch its face, stroke its long hair. But she doesn't move. She just looks at it. She just looks at the face and the hair that are actually hers.

Yasmine opens her eyes, escaping the nightmarish scene, landing straight into the confusion of abrupt awakenings. The room is mostly dark, shadows overlapping shadows, and the faintest hints of light coming shyly through the windows. Shaken and too weary to speak, she stares into nothingness, wondering, "What was all this about?"

She could still feel the sense of helplessness that had overwhelmed her just before she opened her eyes, when a fleeting vision of her mother in monstrous guise causes her to shudder and sit up. Hugging her knees, she fixes her gaze on the nightly view afforded through the window panes and, thinking, "…just a dream …just a dream," tries to forget, partly hoping to be right, partly prodding nervously in search of a satisfying explanation.

Sitting in darkness, Lalla Amina stares through the glass door that leads to her garden. In the silence of a house that seems too large now that she has no one but Batoul to share it with, she cannot help but feel lonely and lost. She wishes for someone to hold her, for someone to care. She's exhausted, unable sleep. Paulo's words, still pressing heavily against her chest, have brought out too many questions, too many ifs; ifs that go too far back into the past; ifs that force her to remember very distant years, when a young man, walked into her home, accompanied by a father who was to meet up with hers.

On that unforgettable day, she had been reading a Jules Verne's novel, in the shade of a fig tree, when the two strangers shook hands with her father, and followed him into his study. It was 1953 and her country was occupied by both France and Spain, with France holding the lion's share. She had known that her father, Haj Nasr Berrada, a distinguished lawyer and prominent figure in the intellectual struggle for independence, was also secretly involved in the underground insurgent movement that fought for Morocco's liberation, but had never tried to find out more about his activities.

However, that afternoon, feeling inspired by Verne's adventurous tale, she put her book down and walked toward her father's private office. But, as she neared the door against which she had planned on pressing her ear for an exciting session of ease-dropping, the young visitor came out, giving her a fright to remember, and ruining her sleuthing efforts.

He said hello as if nothing had happened, as if everything was at it should be. Brooding silently, she nodded. He averted his eyes and stiffened a bit, looking highly uncomfortable. She guessed he was the shy type and wondered if he was waiting for her to go away. Amina smirked. Now that she was aware of his nervousness, she was set on remaining where she was. After a short silence, he glanced at her and strained to smile. She smiled back in a knowing sort of way and said, "My name is Amina."

For a second, his green eyes glistened, reflecting the sun shining behind her, before he gazed down at his shoes.

She prodded, "What is your name?"

He fidgeted and replied, "Isaam."

Amina grinned and said, "You're not from Fez, are you?"

Isaam shook his head and glanced back at the door, as if worried that one of the two men inside might be standing behind him and said, "I'm from Oujda"

Amina looked at his modest clothes, his dirt covered

shoes, and sighed, "You're quite a ways from Oujda. What are you doing so far from your home?"

Isaam, noticing that she was examining him, looked her up and down and sneered, "My family is moving here."

Amina nodded and moved closer, hoping to startle him, the way beautiful female characters manage to, in the French novels she was forbidden to read but read anyway, and asked, "How do you know my father?"

Isaam shrugged his shoulders, "He's a friend of my father."

Amina raised an eyebrow, "What does your father do again?"

He shook his head, "I never told you."

Amina took another step toward the young man, whose proximity, for reasons she couldn't comprehend yet, was causing her to feel very warm and tingly. She grinned, "Is it a secret?"

He frowned and stared at her from beneath his thick eyebrows and said, "No. And why are you asking anyway?"

Amina tilted her head, crossed her arms and asked, "Two strangers walk into my house... shouldn't I know who they are and what their purpose is?"

Isaam shook his head, "Curiosity can be unhealthy."

"Not as much as secrecy," winked Amina.

The young man took a deep breath and was about to say something, probably pertaining to what he thought of her questions, but the door opened up and her father walked out, followed by his.

Haj Nasr stared at his daughter and then at Isaam.

Amina smiled innocently. Isaam, on the other hand, couldn't help but blush, while shifting on his feet.

"Amina," remarked her father, an amused grin on his face, "I see that you've met one of our new neighbors."

"Neighbors?"

"Yes, the Jazils are moving to the house next door."

"Really?"

"Yes. We are renting it to Haj Abdullah here," he said, pointing to the man with a sharp face, a curved blade for a nose, and green piercing eyes.

"Good," nodded Amina, trying to keep her eyes from the secretive boy who had unexpectedly entered her life. Then, excusing herself, she headed back to the fig tree and its cool shade to be alone, fully aware that on that day she would find herself unable to resist thinking about her new neighbor, unaware that a few months later, and after a dozen not-so-accidental encounters, they would profess the depth of their attraction and desire for each other, in the sheltering peacefulness of her garden, between a fig tree and a rosebush.

Thus, and from then on, she began waiting for his visits, praying for his safe return from whatever missions her father, as she had come to understand, used to mastermind. Worriedly, she counted the days until they could meet to dream and talk about the future, about starting a family in an independent Morocco, and having children who would be given the great privilege and right of growing and prospering in a free land.

Inspired by the warmth of their feelings, they imagined themselves, as a united couple, traveling wherever they pleased inside a country they deeply cherished. They thought they would be able to marry, blessed by both parents. They thought they would meet the world as one, their path strewn with joy and happiness.

Remembering, Lalla Amina feels bitterness rising from within, as she comes face to face with what might have been but wasn't, the thick shadow of dreams that never came true, the burden of loss...

She sighs and nods in silence, remembering being too young and too naïve. She recalls the foolishness of her desires, at a time when she was so confident about the righteousness of her feelings that she actually went ahead and confided in her mother -the woman whom she was certain would understand and support her, the only person that could have influenced her father's decision when the appropriate time came for her loved one to ask for her hand.

Amina could never forget her mother's smile, fake and distant. She could never forget how Isaam disappeared afterwards. Nor, would she forget how her mother, oblivious to her sorrow, went ahead and invited a young Fassi, from a very prestigious family, a man with a promising future, a potential husband she was not allowed to refuse.

She could never forget how she wanted to run away -had only her beloved returned. But the beloved never came back. No, he simply vanished out of her existence. The house next door became a vacant space again, and the Jazils' were nowhere to be seen or found. It was as if they had never existed, as if they had been a mere figment of her boundless imagination.

Of course, she tried to stand strong and wait for Isaam, clinging dearly to hopeless hope, but her father had a different plan, and she, a respectable young woman born to a world of men, couldn't go against her father's wishes. So, she lowered her head and surrendered to her fate. There was a huge wedding and a lot of fake smiles. That night, with a band playing, and guests clapping, she cried, and smiled. She said farewell to Isaam's memory, and swore that if she ever had a daughter, she would never do what her mother had done. She would never break her own child's heart.

In the silence of a dark lonely night, Lalla Amina thinks of the daughter she betrayed and the promise she broke. She feels the scolding breath of guilt over her burdened conscience. Succumbing to remorse, she begins to cry and pray for forgiveness.

Yasmine wakes up the next morning slightly after four. She opens he eyes to the darkness that has for hours now filled her bedroom. She sits up and slowly walks out to the section of the living room she uses as a study. Despite the early hour and the prevailing darkness, she is aware of a feeling of great clarity within. She takes a seat at her desk and starts thinking about the conversation she had with Paulo Aduro, playing it, over and over again, in her head, trying to make sense out of it, until a decision is formed. Then, she gets up, takes a shower, gets dressed, and sits at the kitchen's table, in front of a steaming cup of instant Nescafe, with a pen and a blank piece of paper, to write everything she will have to do.

She arrives to her practice an hour earlier than usual and has to unlock the door. No one is inside. She passes Aicha's still vacant desk and enters her office, her sanctuary. She opens all curtains and windows, inviting in both light and fresh air.

She sits at her desk, opens her briefcase and pulls out the list she's made earlier, unfolds it, and begins comparing its content with that of her time planner to find that she is working on twenty six cases all due in the next thirty days, in addition to the usual monthly work load dealing with administrative reports, and a few consulting projects for certain firms and clients her practice handles.

At twenty past eight, Aicha arrives to find the office's main door unlocked, and immediately guesses that Yasmine is inside, which in its self is not that unusual. She walk in, sets her purse in one of her desk's drawers, turns on her electrical typewriter, opens a few windows, unlocks a couple of doors and then goes to check on her boss who asks her to come in, close the door and have a seat.

"Aicha, I will be taking a break from work in fifteen days. I have made a list of what needs to be done in my absence," she hands her a sheet of paper, "I will handle all the cases that are due in court until I am ready to leave. All the remaining cases, highlighted on the list, as well as any new ones, will have to be taken by Touria; I will let her know as soon as she arrives."

After giving Aicha a moment to examine the list, she resumes, setting her gaze on the section of blue sky that fills her window view, "I am certain Touria will not object. I have covered for her whenever she needed me to." Then turning to face her secretary, allows a smile, "Plus, you are very familiar will all the files and their contents; I trust that the transfer should occur very smoothly."

Looking rather surprised, the secretary leans forward and asks, "Is everything alright, Madame?"

"Y-yes, I just have a personal matter that I need to attend to," as Yasmine's eyes return to the window, surrendering to blue nothingness, she is unable to keep her mind from drifting away, and down, to a beach where she hopes to put an end to that recurring dream of hers, until a question brings her wandering attention back to her assistant.

"Are there any travel arrangements you would like me to handle for you?"

Yasmine nods appreciatively, "Not yet Aicha. I will let you know when I'm ready." Then rubs her hands together, she exclaims, "Well now. It is time to get some work done."

Touria, an old friend from law school with whom Yasmine had graduated, as well as the partner with whom she had opened the practice, is thrilled upon hearing that Yasmine is finally willing to take a break, a 'well-deserved break,' as she puts it.

She even demands from Yasmine to go on and have as much fun as she can, adding, "Stay there until you recharge your batteries and do not come back until you get a beautiful tan, and perhaps one of those uplifting torrid affairs that come with the spontaneity of adventure."

Yasmine laughs and replies, "I'll try my best, and we'll see what happens."

"No, no… I want you to do more than try. I want you to make things happen," she get off her chair and walks around her desk to give her friend a big hug with a kiss on each cheek. When she lets go of Yasmine, a warm smile is permeating her facial expression, and softening her calculating eyes.

Yasmine takes a deep breath and thanks Touria for her understanding, only to be answered with a dismissive wave of the hand. On her way out, she says, "I'll bring you something nice."

"You know me. I'm always happy to get good chocolate, or wine," replies the business partner, "Then again, just come back happy."

When Lalla Amina phones and asks to speak with her daughter, Yasmine is so consumed by her decision, so excited by the prospect of taking a break, that she doesn't hesitate to take the call, "Hello mother, how are you?"

"I'm alright… " Lalla Amina's voice comes out broken, as if it were riddled with nervousness, "Yes, I'm fine."

"Are you sure?" Yasmine barely recognizes her mother.

"Yes… But, how are you?"

"Actually, I'm feeling very well today. I had an excellent time last night. Thank you so much for inviting me."

"Oh… I'm really glad you enjoyed it."

"Mother, are you sure you're okay?"

"I'm fine. I'm fine…" responds Lalla Amina evasively, before inquiring, "Yasmine, what did you talk about with Mr. Aduro?"

"Nothing, we just chatted… You know, we walked around the garden and came back inside."

"Did he… eh… say something about me?" Lalla Amina's sounds weak and worried.

"Why would he talk about you?"

"I don't know… I don't know!" she protests, sounding rather unsettled.

"I am really getting worried now."

"I'm fine, I swear… Anyway, I just called to see how you were doing. And…" she pauses, her words lose whatever little credibility they could have had, before adding, "Yasmine, I'm sure you're busy, right now… so, I'll just let you get back to work."

"Mother, actually, I am glad you called. I have a favor

to ask from you," Yasmine puts down the pen she is rolling between her fingertips.

"What is it, Princess?" her mother tries to sound cheerful.

"I've decided to take a break from work and go on a short sort of vacation… you know, to relax a little."

"Excellent. You and Adil really need it."

"No, no, mother," she corrects, "Adil will not be coming."

"What do you mean?"

Yasmine peers through the window, sees two birds flying by, and wishes she could be one of them, "I am going alone."

"Alone?"

Yasmine pictures her mother shaking her head in disbelief, "Yes. Alone."

"Oh, I see… Sure. Hmm. I guess. Yes. Well, and what do you need?"

"I plan on visiting Spain, and I was wondering if you were still in good terms with the Spanish consul's wife. You know how long the lines can be for visas," Yasmine sighs at the thought of a large crowd sadly camping outside every European consulate overnight, sometimes days at a time, just to try their luck at a chance to leave the country.

"Sure honey. I see Madame Cortez at the tennis club all the time. Just send me your passport and leave the rest to me."

"Thank you mother, I really appreciate this."

"Oh, it's no big deal. Don't you worry about it."

"Wonderful."

"And Yasmine, do you think that we could get together... I would love to talk to you."

"Sure, but I'm somewhat busy right now. How about after I return?"

"S-sure... It sounds perfect."

"I'll phone you as soon as I come back.'

"Good."

"Mother?"

"Yes, dear."

"I just want you to know that I love you... and I'm very sorry for all the times I wasn't able to show it to you." Yasmine waits a response, but none comes. "Mother..." and hears a sniffle.

"I-I love you too, Yasmine." Lalla Amina responds with a voice that seems to be soaked with emotional warmth.

"Have a good day now, okay?"

"I'll talk to you later... Take care."

"You too. Bye."

"Bye."

Yasmine hangs up, surprisingly pleased by the unexpected warmth she is feeling for her mother. Then, looking at the phone, she remembers that she has to call Adil in his office, to let him know about her plans, just in case her mother tries reaching him to check on how he feels about his wife traveling alone. Slowly, she reaches for the handle, picks it up and, hesitantly, dials his office number.

"Doctor Khadir's office, how may I assist you?"

"Hello Najat, this is Yasmine."

"Oh, hello Madame Berrada," the voice sounding cold, almost hostile, inquires, "What can I do for you?"

"Could I speak to Adil, if he isn't too busy?" Yasmine bites her lower lip, hopeful that once she lets Adil know about her plans he will be smart enough to put two and two together, and come to the conclusion that something important is happening to his wife. Maybe, she prays. Maybe, he'll even foresee that this trip of hers, so unusual and unprecedented, is in fact the beginning of the end of whatever is still holding them together.

She sees him, facing life in its undeniable truth, deprived of the fake partner and accomplice in whom he has been blaming all his woes and miseries, and thus having no other choice but that of doing the right thing and starting anew. Yes, starting anew, she imagines, as soon as they finish talking and hang up on each other, because he will decide right there and then to follow his heart.

"I am afraid that Ad…" the receiver buzzes with discomfort, "Doctor Khadir is in the middle of taking a patient's x-rays. Would you like him to call you back, or would you prefer holding until he is done?"

"I would rather have him…" Yasmine pauses, and listens to Nadia's breathing. She hears the confirmation of what she has suspected for many years now. She hears, or rather feels, frustration and jealousy. It all so clear, and so vivid, that empathy fills her heart and rushes through her lips.

"You know what…" she looks at the ceiling, "just tell him that I will be going on a trip out of the country in fifteen days."

Taken by surprise, Najat doesn't answer. Her mind is swept in a flood of silenced speculations upon many a convenient reason behind Yasmine's words, so much so that she is startled when Yasmine's voice calls her, "Najat, are you there?"

A nervous smile forms on the desperate lover's lips, "Of... course, Madame. I will let Doctor Khadir know. Is there anything else I can help you with?"

The attorney, as if she were able to see the woman her husband has been for too long wishing to, silently and secretly, be with, smiles back, "No... actually, yes. Could you tell him that I am planning on going to Spain?"

"Of course Madame, I will transmit the message to Doctor Khadir as soon as he is finished with his patient," Najat's tone changes suddenly, betraying, if anything then, a great deal of exhilaration.

Yasmine grins, feeling rather satisfied, as if she's just fixed an old wrong, "Thank you Najat," She grins and relaxes as some old tension she didn't even realize was there lets go of her chest, of her mind, "thank you for everything."

"You're..." Najat taken aback, stutters her reply, "... welcome, Madame. And have a safe trip."

"Take care of yourself Najat." Yasmine hangs up, leans on her chair, looking outside, feeling as light as the fluffy clouds of her childhood dreams seemed to have been. Gazing at the sky, she lets go and dreams of escape.

Maria Santiago was a strong woman, a southern woman, who, from a very early age, had learned to accept life's harshness, and to always be ready for the worst. Born in a small village on the coast of Andalusia, to a family of fishermen and hard working women, she had seen her father sail into a brooding sea, under darkly ominous clouds, to never come back again. She had discovered grief and, soon after, poverty —as they sought her at too young an age. She had watched her mother struggle for her family's survival. She had experienced hunger, alongside her three younger sisters, and learned to ignore and even laugh at its gnawing company.

Luckily, Maria Santiago was a born fighter. Like her mother, she resisted the downward pull of too many wants and did her best to keep her spirit high. Seeking life's silver lining no matter how grim the situation confronting her, she worked hard and sang, letting her naturally melodious voice carry her past the constraints harsh fate thrust her way during the sunlit hours of her days. Then, whenever day gave way to night, She would be found, clad in her most beautiful dress and favorite pair of shoes, dancing flamenco, stomping her feet, releasing the frustration which source was a deep felling of helplessness that seemed to ebb and flow as if effected by the waning and waxing of the moon, the sun and who knows what other celestial bodies.

In those nights, Maria Santiago standing tall and undaunted, shoulders rolled back, showing pride in her womanhood, in her bloodline, in her peoples' history. She faced life with passion and pride, daring the world with her gaze and the assertiveness of her body's expressiveness, drawing respect from all those who could see her, being an inspiration to her peers, as if embodying the often muffled and suppressed, warrior goddess that dwells in every woman, a living representation of grace and courage.

On her seventeenth spring, Maria Santiago gathered her clothes in a second-hand suitcase, she had purchased from an old man at the local market —a warm face that wished her good luck. Then, she went to find her mother, Sabrina the widow, to hug her goodbye and to tell her not to worry, not to cry, to believe that good things will come, to trust fate and to light a candle by the virgin's feet and pray for her daughter's wellbeing. She promised the woman who taught her everything and raised her to be the decent person she had become, that she would take care of herself and that she wouldn't forget her family. She promised that she would send them money and swore that she would come back, whenever the chance presented itself.

Later that day, she kissed her sisters and climbed inside a bus headed for Bilbao. She waved them good-bye, until they disappeared, along with the bus station on which platform they were standing, and then allowed herself to finally fall apart. She allowed herself to cry, surrendering to fear and uncertainty -both born to the prospect of launching forward, with nothing but the unknown ahead of her.

Maria Santiago traveled north, crossing the country she had been born to -one she never had the chance to see- seated on a packed bus that would not cease humming a mechanically numbing tune as long as it was rolling forth, following dizzyingly snaking roads that cut through the bustling cities, smaller towns and quiet villages, before unwinding into rural wilderness, streaming along unfolding valleys, rolling hills, trees solemnly standing in long files that stretched for acres aside green grassy pastures and bare soil, until arriving to her destination.

Bilbao, a northern city she had heard many good things about, a place, and so was the common belief, where people could work and earn a living, build something for the future, for the coming days when the body turns frail and becomes highly susceptible to all sorts of incapacitating illnesses.

The bus entered this city of great hopes on a busy afternoon, right as siesta time was coming to end, with stores reopening their front doors -a good omen, thought Maria Santiago, as a burst of excitement ran through her body and made her fidget on the seat she was beginning to believe had become glued to her bottom.

Nervously, she straightened her back and stretched her neck to see what was happening outside. She found sidewalks filled with pedestrians wearing all sorts of dresses, uniforms and vests and matching pants -mostly dark colors, mopeds and cars, (French, Italian, Swedish, and German, in red, black, white, yellow, and blue...) zooming through the streets, honking and puffing smoke every now and then.

She imagined herself belonging to this world, so different from anything she had known until that moment, with all its buildings and streets, storefronts and balconies, cement and asphalt. She scanned through the faces of strangers as they crossed her path, looking for hints of the familiar, for a smile, a nod, or any other gesture that could be interpreted as a welcoming sign, meeting nothing but grim faces, heads looking down, people, men and women, living in the same bustling city, and yet completely lost in their own heads, disconnected from those with whom they were actually sharing everything, every minute of everyday, as if they had chosen to wear the very cloak of deep loneliness, to go on being disengaged, and uncaring.

Suddenly, the bus stopped at a busy intersection, right in front of the window of a grocer's store. She tried too see inside, but instead recognized her own reflection on the display window. She looked exhausted and lost. She forced a smile nonetheless, and smiling found warmth in her mirror image, which, having nothing else to hold on to, she chose to take as a sign beckoning her to go on, encouraging her to be strong and brave. She saw hope, and that was all she needed to believe she would make it.

At the station, she got off the bus and was handed her old-but-sturdy suitcase, took a deep breath, straightened her gait and took another step forward seeking her destiny.

From then on, unwilling to take no for an answer, no matter how many nos she'd heard, knocking on doors, no matter how many unopened, or slammed shut ones she came upon, Maria Santiago forged ahead. Despite the grim prospects of what tomorrows might bring, she persisted, carried by shear stubbornness and desperation, until she was able to settle down and begin a new life, one that led her to learn the meaning of loneliness, of longing, and of nostalgia.

No matter how strong, Maria still ached for her mother's comforting words. She longed for her sisters' presence. She missed her people and that village of hers, with its every road and wall. She even missed that treacherous Mediterranean Sea. Yet, there was no turning back for her. She had to stay, and could not afford being weak, despite the locals' cold looks and scornful words –those that draw out late night tears and sorrow. She had to stay. So she stayed, worked hard and saved every peseta she could manage to keep away from the unavoidable cold blooded bill collectors.

She lived a frivolous life, eating once a day, and refraining from ever buying new clothes. However once a month, she could be seen walking to the post office, her face brightly lit with deeply felt pride for being able to send a check to her mother. On those cherished days, Maria moved completely inspired by the warming fact that she was keeping a promise she had made to the woman who had deprived herself for too long to feed her children.

On those days, Maria could never resist feeling elated for being able to give back to the one who worked so hard and so much to keep her daughters healthy and warm, wearing herself out on the way, as she tried her hardest to give them all the things she hadn't received as a child, just to see them laugh and smile, just to have them grow in decency.

Maria Santiago continued thus, for two years, struggling to get herself out of misery's reach, fighting battle after battle, never losing sight of what she truly desired, seeing every day gone as another step taken to bring her closer to fulfilling her goals and dreams, and meeting every moment of her life full of undeterred hope. Until, a few pesetas became more than she could have ever imagined being able to hold, until not much became something… a little van and a small trailer, which she kept packed with snacks she sold at the doors of nearby factories.

It was right then, and just as life was beginning to smile at her, that Alberto showed up, perhaps because life never goes the way one plans it. Alberto appeared on one of those hot summer days, when streets tend to shimmer under a burning sun, while the air is turned into hot ascending veils of vapor, nets of viscous ether that neither breeze nor wind can breach. There, in front of her van, he stood, the top two buttons of his white shirt opened, broad chest revealed, his sleeves rolled up to the elbows, and started handing pamphlets to the workers who were walking out.

Alberto walked to Maria, wearing a proud smile on his face, and handed her one of his pamphlets. His eyes looked into hers. They touched her face and reached for her heart. She blushed and tried to smile back. He tilted his head, nodded and left her, retracing his steps toward the factory's entrance.

That day, she listened to him talk with passion about rights and justice. She felt his voice throb in her ears, and lost herself to the sweetness of the awakened sensation. She stared at him from a distance, behind a crowd that had begun gathering pulled by his speech. She lingered on his features and on his eyes, oblivious to the rest, suspended in a dream at the edge of reality, until the police arrived, their vans covering his voice with the deafening sound of their piercing sirens.

The crowd dispersed, and Alberto vanished. He disappeared, in ruckus and confusion, unaware that, on the deserted street, the woman who had quieted his mind with the softness of her eyes, was feeling cold and confused, wondering if she was actually dreaming, while dearly holding on to a pamphlet so as not to lose her mind, so as to never forget.

That night, she dreamt of him and of his voice. She woke up sweating in the darkness of her studio apartment, opened the bedroom window and sat on its wooden ledge, staring at the empty street three floors below, crazy thoughts slipping through her mind. She thought of looking for him, but then laughed for having such a childish idea. Yet, despite her dismissive reaction, Maria could not get the rubble rouser out of her head. He insisted on haunting her, even as the sun arose one more time, and as the night was pushed aside.

Obsessed she remained, while time passed, sun and moon revolving along fated tracks stretching through the heavens above, their motion effecting tides and moods alike, as they went on imposing their circadian rhythms on everything organic and alive. In fact, as time trickled forth, her inexplicable wish to find this mysterious man was actually growing in intensity, until she could no longer ignore it.

Unable to muffle the pressing urgency of a pulsating desire that was incessantly drumming from too deep within, caught in a wave of passion that had risen too high and was about to break, Maria Santiago surrendered and began listening to her heart.

Thus and without a month gone, Maria began looking for Alberto. It started on a Tuesday morning, at a time when she was supposed to already be on the road. On that morning, Maria was staring at her coffee, sitting on the only chair she owned. She had pulled the pamphlet -the only proof she had of his existence- out of the kitchen cabinet where she had been keeping it, and was presently reading its content. She read it a dozen times looking for clues, and could find none, but the address of the regional labor union. She put the pamphlet in her coat's inner pocket and walked out of her building determined to act. She went to the train station and bought a ticket to San Sebastian –the rebel city.

Three hours later, she was threading through streets she had never visited. She stopped at cafes, with the pamphlet in hand, and asked questions that no one was willing to answer. She ignored the suspicious looks that people seemed too eager to cast upon her. Pretending not to worry that someone might suspect her of being a Spanish spy, dismissing her fears of what might happen, she followed her heart, even as her heart insisted on putting her in a very precarious position.

Maria knew very well that these people were fighting for their independence. They had never seen themselves as part of the Spanish state. They were Basque and wanted to remain so. They stood up to Franco, called him an unjust ruler, as in their eyes, he stubbornly insisted on seeing them subjugated and refused to see how primordial autonomy was to them. They saw Franco as an evil dictator, a mass murderer whom they would never forgive for the massacre of Guarnica.

How could they forget Guarnica? Those who had fallen that day were innocent and defenseless civilians, mainly children and women. They never had a chance against the German fighter aircrafts the monster had called upon to show his might. Perhaps, he was so blind that he really believed that unrestrained brutality could tame the region and force the Basques into submission. Perhaps, he didn't realize that they would refuse to surrender to his bigotry, or that they would resist and fight, despite the waves of arrests that swept over their communities and families, despite the turmoil he would bring upon their land and lives. Yet, no matter what Franco did, Spaniards were Spaniards, and Basques were Basques. It had been so for over a thousand years. It was a matter of blood, a matter for which lives had been and still would be taken. Maria knew all this, yet she had to keep on trying her luck.

When the night caught up with her, she sought refuge in an old pension, where she slept with a knife under the pillow. The next morning, after having gone through the regional phone book, she hit the streets again, and headed to one of the many trade union offices located in San Sebastian.

Inside the union's two story building, she showed a burly front desk clerk, built more like a wrestler than a clerk, the pamphlet and asked to see the man who had been distributing them at the factory's door. The clerk eyed her silently for a moment, while playing with his thick moustache, and then asked her to provide him with a reason for such an unusual request. She fidgeted on her feet and attempted to explain that it was personal. He raised a thick eyebrow and let her know that there was no way for him, or anyone else, in the building, to provide her with a name. He apologized and pointed to the door.

Maria wouldn't leave. She insisted on getting an answer, on the grounds that it was a matter of life and death. He shook his head and told her to go home. She asked him if there were any open positions at the union. He laughed, leaned back on his chair and started speaking his peoples' language. She let him know that she didn't understand Basque that well. He nodded, as if having proved a point, and let her know that everyone here was a volunteer. She told him that she wanted to volunteer. He looked at her through narrow eyes, leaned forward and asked her who had sent her to the union. She replied that no one had.

The bulky receptionist resumed playing with his moustache, while looking at the pamphlet. She continued looking him in the eyes, defiant and unflinching. Suddenly, the man allowed what resembled a friendly grin and suggested that she comes back the following night, at eight o'clock in the evening. She smiled with all of her heart and thanked him. Without a reply, he grabbed a newspaper that was sitting, unfolded, on his desk, and began reading. When Maria left the building, the man at the desk reached for the telephone, dialed a number, and began gently tapping the thumb of his free hand on his desk, while waiting for someone to answer.

Upon her return the next evening, a man was waiting for her, barely visible where he stood in the shadows that surrounded the dimly lighted clerk's desk. He asked her if she had come alone. She said, yes. He asked her if anyone knew where she was. She said, no. He moved closer to the only flickering light in the room, and until she could discern some of his features. Looking at her, he smiled, revealing a broken tooth, and suggested that if he were to kill her and properly dispose of her body, no one would ever know what had happened to her.

With a chill running through her body, Maria nodded, yes, and squeezed the handle of the knife she was holding in the hand kept concealed behind the large black purse she had been clasping since her arrival. She stood still and tried to avoid showing any sign of fear, which was rather hard under the circumstances. He moved away from the light, becoming a dark shadow, and asked her why she was looking for the fellow who was distributing the pamphlets. She answered that it was personal. He reached into his jacket's side-pockets, paused for a second, his dark eyes fixating hers, before pulling out a crumbled pack of cigarettes from one and a box of matches from the other, and then said that he might be able to help her if she were to share her reasons for being so dangerously nosy, and stopped being so secretive about the nature of her intentions.

Maria looked at her interrogator and insisted that her reasons were personal and that she could only share them with the one she was looking for. With a cigarette in his mouth and a burning match lighting up his face, he asked her what she would do if he couldn't help her. She said that she didn't know, that she might come back the next day to stand by the union's door and wait for the man she was looking for to show up.

"Why?" The question came from behind her. She spun around and saw a dark silhouette standing by the door.

"Who are you?" she asked.

There was a pause, then, "I recognize you…"

She moved toward the voice she was recognizing, "It's you, isn't it?"

He said, "…two weeks ago, in Bilbao, right?"

She walked into the darkness where he was hiding and reached for his face. He felt her hand as it touched his lips. She took a deep breath and asked, "What's your name?"

He swallowed nervously, causing his Adam's apple to move up and down, and then replied, "Al-berto."

She repeated, "Alberto," while moving her fingers along his cheek bone.

Ignoring the sound of laughter coming from the man who had been questioning her, Alberto asked, "Are you alright?"

Relieved, Maria answered, "Yes, I think so."

For two weeks now, Yasmine has been searching desperately for any information on the village with no name, or anything related to the mentioned mural facing the sea. She has been searching, but to no avail. Every evening after work, she has been rushing back home, where the walls are plastered with Post-it notes, and the living room floor and table engulfed under a carpet of maps, brochures and open books -all replete with data related to Andalusia.

Barely allowing time for a quick shower, a bite to eat, she's been diving, undeterred, into a sea of facts, hunting for cogent clues leading to Esperanza, finding nothing cardinal to get her hands on.

Tonight however, she is sitting on the coach, face drawn, preoccupied by the fact that tomorrow she is supposed to be catching a flight. Her airline ticket is ready, along with visa and rental car reservation. Everything is in the side pocket of a small traveling bag laden with the essentials she plans to keep with her at all times. The clothes she's selected for the trip are neatly packed in a larger bag. Everything is ready, except, except Yasmine.

"If only I knew where I was going exactly?" she examines her notes, desperately trying to find some piece of evidence that might have eluded her during her prior searches. Andalusia, she reads, was named so by the Arabs when they controlled the region. It stretches through a rather large area in the south of Spain, running along the Mediterranean, the Atlantic, and the Portuguese south eastern border, all the way to the Spanish provinces of Albacete and Murcia to the East, and Badojor and New Castile to the North.

Exasperated, Yasmine huffs loudly. Once again, there is nothing to be found. She throws the useless book on the floor and holds her head between her two hands, pressing hard on her temples, attempting to squeeze out a brooding feeling of frustration that has taken hold of her as soon as she started dealing with the illogical, as soon as she allowed herself to step into the unknown. She groans as her eyes settle over the mess she's made thus far in the apartment.

Deciding to do something about it, she starts cleaning the leaving room, removing the Post-it notes from the walls, the television, the framed art-deco pictures, the coffee table, the sofa. She picks up all of the books and the maps, along with the heaps of paper she finds strewn in no logical order on the floor.

Done tidying the place, she collapses, exhausted, onto the sofa and, closing her eyes, finds that her mind has become much calmer, ready to review all that she's learned one last time. Keeping her eyes shut, breathing slowly, consciously, she begins seeing that her area of interest, as daunting as it stands, can be narrowed to a specific stretch of the Mediterranean coast, starting from the city of Tarifa and ending at Nerja.

"Still," she reflects, "There remains too many small villages scattered along that section of the coast to be checked, and what if the one I am looking for is at the end of the road.

" Yasmine sighs, reawakened frustration regaining the upper hand against her better judgment, quickly darkening her mood. "There is no way to determine how much time this crazy adventure will take. No way."

She presses the heels of her palms against her eye sockets. "What has to be done has to be done, and that's that." Feeling weak, her arms relax. Her back surrenders to the couch's softness, "I need to stop worrying."

Biting her lips, she wonders, "Why am I so scared? This is absurd."

Anger like a volcano erupts within. She straightens her spine and slaps the cushion she has sunk in, "Enough is enough already!"

Brushing aside every single doubt she has been wrestling with at once, she decides that her situation, no matter how unclear at the moment, is rather manageable. Somewhat satisfied, she nods silently —to set the record straight, once and for all, letting both conscious and subconscious minds know that she, Yasmine Berrada adamantly refuses to give up.

But Time never denied, like a wheel on which spokes this world of ours in its entirety is fastened, forever spinning, leads us in circles from twin pearly bead to twin pearly bead, on an seemingly endless necklace of identical cycles.

Thus, at nine o'clock in the evening, twelve hours from departure time, sitting at the kitchen table, vaguely staring at a glass of milk she has barely touched, with worry inundating her thoughts, painting the whole idea into a huge mistake, Yasmine, once again, feels embarrassed for having allowed herself to be influenced by an old fool, and why not a charlatan. For all she knows, the man could be deranged. "Stupid, that's what I am." She hides her face in her hands, heavily leaning with her elbows on the table.

Lost in self-deprecation, she is startled by the sound of the door opening, and quickly lifts her head up. Adil walks in, much earlier than usual. He says hi, sets his briefcase against the wall, takes off his jacket and joins her at the table.

"Are you excited?" he smiles, looking happier than he'd ever been since she'd known him, "Tomorrow, you will be in Spain."

Silently, she fakes an acquiescing look and touches the glass in front of her, all the while wondering if it is expectation of sweet things to come she sees glowing through his face, "I'm thinking about canceling the whole thing."

Adil's eyes widen, "Are you kidding me?"

She pushes the glass away from her, "No, I don't think it's a good idea."

Looking rather confused, Adil asks, "Why?"

She looks away, "Like I said, it doesn't' look like a good idea anymore."

Adil loosens his tie, pulls out a chair, and joins her at the table, "Is it because of your work?"

"That's one of many reasons that come to mind," she grabs the glass of milk, stands up, walks to the sink, dumps its lukewarm contents, and starts washing it.

Staring at her back, distressed by her change of heart, he remarks, "Work can wait."

She looks up and sighs, "I know."

"Yasmine," he stands up, "to be honest with you, I was looking forward to your departure."

She smirks and turns off the water, "Really?"

He walks around the table and joins her by the sink, "I need time to… think."

She turns to face him. But as soon as their eyes meet, he looks the other way, as if to hide the obviousness of his feelings. But Yasmine isn't blind to how exhausted he is, how miserable he's been —she knows because she feels the same way too. Her face softens, "I know the feeling."

Adil exhales slowly and then says, "Then, you should go."

She smiles tenderly and nods, "You're probably right. I will go."

"What are you doing?" asked Caesar shyly.

"I'm drawing the outline of a guitar," replied Andalou with a smile.

"A real guitar?"

"Yes," nodded Andalou.

The boy's eyes widen, "Have you ever made one before?"

"No, this is the first one." Curious, Caesar climbed on a high chair to get a better view of his uncle's work bench, observed him for a little while, and then asked, "Who is it for?"

"No one, really… just something I've wanted to do, for a long time."

"Do you know how to play?"

"A little, your father taught me how to play a few songs."

Caesar focused his gaze on the drawing, examining it silently, and then inquired, "Could you teach me?"

Of course, I'd love to," he nodded and, glancing thoughtfully at the young boy, added, "Actually, I'll make you a guitar of your own. What do you say?"

Caesar's face lit with unmistakable joy, "Really?" Excitedly, he leaned over the bench and offered, "Can I help you make it?"

"Of course," replied Andalou, while reaching for a plastic protractor and a wooden fifty centimeters long ruler, "we can start as soon as I finish this one."

"Great!" Caesar bounced a few times on his chair.

Andalou laughed and shook his head, "And how was school?"

"Good," answered Caesar with a slight frown.

"Hah, I'm guessing that you got your scores on the

last test back…" Andalou was measuring lines and angles he had already drawn over wooden sheets about to be made into something different and functional.

"Yes," responded the boy with a sigh.

"And? How did you do?"

"I got the third highest score in the class," complained Caesar.

The wood carver whistled, "That's very good."

Caesar nodded unconvincingly, "I could have done better…"

Andalou closed one eye and gave the dissatisfied boy a sly look with the other, "Did Lola do better than you again?"

"Yes," confessed Caesar with a huff.

"Do you know what I think?"

"I don't like her!"

"If you say so."

"I don't," insisted the boy

"Not even a little?"

Caesar was blushing, "No!"

Andalou shook his head, "I don't know…"

"Ahhh!" Caesar raised his arms, giving up, and then jumped down, lip curled in frustration, "I'm going to go do my homework."

Andalou chuckled, "Caesar, Do you feel like playing a game of football later?"

The boy nodded, "Oh, yes."

"Good. Come and get me when you're done, okay?"

"Okay," said Caesar, and, without a second's hesitation, dashed out of the workshop.

It is almost noon when Yasmine arrives in Seville. She finds it simmering under a bright and intrusive sun whose light seems to be oppressing the entire city, summoning steaming vapors from the streets, and pressing people into clusters of desperate sweat dampened figures trying their best to hide in whatever shaded areas they can come across.

She quickly gets in the rental car -a small lime green convertible Volkswagen bug, takes the sunglasses she is wearing off of her face and concentrates on studying the itinerary she had planned and highlighted on a large country map. Then, she pulls a second map —this one, of Seville- out of her small travel bag, and opens it to search and find a way out of the glistening town she had landed in. Finally, after comparing the colored lines on the map to directions she had written inside a small leather bound organizer, she starts the car, shifts into first, listens to the engine as it purrs, and gives it a little gas. With one hand on the steering wheel and the other lightly holding the stick-shift, she takes a deep breath, looking straight ahead, and watches the road and her journey, as they both begin to unfold.

She heads south toward Tarifa, which she reaches late in the evening. There, feeling tired, she decides to stay overnight. The next morning, after a quick breakfast, two slices of bread, butter, preserves and a café con leche, she finds the road closest to the sea and stays on it, heading east.

Sticking to the only plan she could come up with, she goes on stopping at every little town and village she comes by, to ask the same question -tapping into the Spanish lessons she had enjoyed taking in high school and which forgotten fruits seem to be coming back to her- weakly hoping that her inquiry will not prompt the usual negative answer that is always accompanied by looks of mistrust, and that, instead, someone will be able to point her toward the place that haunts her dreams.

After a good twelve hours of searching, feeling abortively exhausted, Yasmine checks in at a very typical Mediterranean auberge, an inn offering rooms with a view on the water, along with delicious dinners served from eight to ten. The owners, a friendly Italian couple who enjoy chatting, greet her warmly, and lead her to her room, a cozy space where she is welcomed by the uplifting scent of jasmine. Once inside and alone, she drops her bags, locks the door, and heads to the bathroom. Closing the door, she lets warm water run, filling the tub, while undressing and untying her hair. Then, one careful foot at a time, she steps into the iron cast tub, immersing her body to the collarbones. Once comfortably settled, she closes her eyes and, surrendering, drifts effortlessly into a restful lull.

There are nights that just aren't meant for sleeping. And this night happens to be one of them for Caesar, as he lies awake, staring through darkness at the ceiling of his room, his mind lost in a stream of memories from days that have passed so long ago. In his head, memories flash at lightening speed, fast-forwarded clips of his short life.

There is his father, Alberto, a stranger, forever distant, a grieving man hiding behind his own silence. Then, there is his mother, Maria, always working, always worried, and most of all always loving. He sees her weakened body lying sick in bed, surrendering slowly to the inevitability of death. He hears her telling him, while stroking his hair, as he sits by her side, that she has to go, that Alberto is waiting for her, that he, Caesar Santiago, will be fine, that Andalou will take care of him, and that she is very, very proud of him.

He feels the tears that once ran down his cheeks, as she tells him that she loves him and wishes him well. He hears his heart beating too fast and his breath running too short. She tells him not too worry and that everything will be fine. She closes her eyes. He remembers kissing her cold hand and sobbing over her lifeless body. He remembers silence in her room. He remembers loss, and a box that has to be buried underground.

Then, he feels Andalou's hand on his shoulder. Andalou, the other stranger, whom he was told to call Uncle Andalou, whom he was supposed to allow into his life, to trust and accept as a father figure, a friend, and a tutor. He remembers Uncle Andalou –the stranger– sitting him down every night, and telling him things. He talks about Alberto. He talks about responsibility and about origins. He speaks of freedom, of people dreaming of independence, of oppression and resistance. He speaks of a language that is as ancient as the history of mankind. He tells him that the people are his people and that the language is his language. And Caesar listens; somehow he doesn't really mind. He listens because he really likes Andalou –the friend. He likes playing soccer with him. He even likes helping him build the woodshop.

Nights like this one, sleepless and endless, are all the same. Nights like this one always come with images of those he loves and cares about. Nights like this one eventually lead him to the woodshop, as it rises, brick by brick, plank by plank, on nothing but sand, out of the barest of grounds. There Esperanza appears, and as soon as she does his mother dies. She dies and leaves him with Andalou; poor uncle Andalou, lost and confused, hiding inside the woodshop to cry.

Afraid of failing, afraid of letting Alberto and Maria down, he cries alone with no one to console him, no one to tell him that it will be alright. Then he comes out and sits with Caesar, pretending to be stronger than he really is, and says, "She is gone to a better place. She is gone to join your Papa."

Nights like this one show him his own face, saddened and lost. He cries and prays. He walks to the sea, the way his mother used to. He holds his hands together and stares at the sky, his mind brimming with hundreds of questions. He wants to know why his father had to die a stranger in his eyes. He wants to know why his mother had to die and leave him behind, deprived of her warm hug, caring gaze, and loving presence. He can't help but think that all of it is his fault. He cries and prays. But the sky remains silent. He cries and prays. He says that

everything is fine when Andalou asks him how he is doing, feeling, or coping. He knows that Andalou is smarter
than that, but he doesn't want the man he calls uncle to
worry because of him. He's so afraid, so afraid of losing
him too.

Nights like this one, bring the sea and the pale moon
to his side, as they come and join him in his mourning
and sorrow. Then, he hears a voice calling him. He turns
and finds Esperanza in a shroud of haze. He looks at her,
bright despite the darkness, and his tears stop falling. He
looks at her, clear in a blurry field, and discovers wonderful truths meant to be reached only through the heart.
He walks to her and touches her feet. He feels soft skin,
radiantly warm, smooth despite the abrasive texture of the
wall she stands against. He raises his eyes and finds those
of a caring soul. She smiles and her smile tells him not to
worry. He smiles and steps back. His eyes let out rivers of
tears, but the tears are those of hope, not of despair. He
walks away and promises himself to always come back.
He walks away knowing that Esperanza will always be
there for him.

Thus, inspired with the faith of the Innocent, free
of doubt, opened to all that could be, welcoming to the
miraculous, the unfunded, drawn beyond the realm of
the proved and ascertained, he gets up every morning and
prays for the memory of his mother, prays for happiness,
prays for warmth and for love.

A knock at the door. Then another. Yasmine forces her eyes open and asks, "Who is it?"

"Dinner is served Signora," a feminine voice replies, in a richly flavored Italian accent.

"Thank you," Yasmine stands up under the shower-head, to wash off the bubbly soap that covers her skin. Then, she steps out of the tub, dries herself with a clean, white towel, before wrapping her hair with another. She leaves the bathroom and sits on the edge of a bed she finds pleasantly soft and rather appealing at this particular moment. For a moment stillness overtakes her. Her mind wonders lightly into semi-nothingness. She drifts, and drifting bumps brushes softly against the idea of dinner, and suddenly, she remembers where she is and what she was doing.

She starts rummaging through the spilled content of the traveling bag lying by her feet and finds what she wants. She springs up, throws on a tee-shirt, slips into a pair of blue jeans, and puts on a pair of white sneakers. Quickly, she checks herself on a tall rectangular mirror hanging against the door, then, dashes out of the room, bounds downstairs. Her hair still wet, feeling refreshed, she joins, in the warmly decorated dinning room, two other guests, a Canadian couple on their twenty-seventh wedding anniversary, and the owners, Eduardo and Francesca, all gathered around a large wooden table, covered with pots, plates, glasses, silverware, a few wine bottles, two large water pitchers, and two round breadbaskets filled to brim.

Famished, Yasmine attacks her food and asks for another helping of the beef and vegetable stew, along with a couple of slices of homemade sourdough bread. She mingles with the sweet Canadian couple, who move her with the love and affection they show each other. Dreamily, she follows them with her eyes as they leave the room romantically holding hands. But once they're gone, reality sets in, and Yasmine becomes painfully aware of the loneliness she carries under her skin. She pours herself a glass of red wine and continues talking to Francesca while watching her clean the large table.

Leaning against a chair and sipping wine, Yasmine learns that Francesca and Ferdinando moved to this area from Lazio on their fifteenth anniversary and never left since. They love each other, with obvious passion, despite their inability to have children, despite both their families' incessant objection to their union, and despite all the hardships life had reserved for them.

Genially, Francesca shares with her guest how she firmly believes that in order for a marriage to work, both partners have to respect, care for, and love one another. They have to be open minded, show patience and be forgiving. Otherwise, tension starts creeping into the relationship, spoiling it from inside, the way a worm does a beautiful apple. Tension, given the chance, becomes a disease that grows into a malignant hatred that eventually abrades whatever household it has managed to enter, bringing about desolation, tainting with unhappiness everything that was good, turning the world sour and making life utterly unbearable.

Yasmine, reminded of her own marriage, finds herself silently entertaining a scenario where, being a more accommodating, flexible, pragmatic wife, she allows her marriage a chance to be saved. Watching the hostess who is setting dirty dishes on the rolling cart, she wonders if she'll ever become as content with life as this settled woman she is looking at through sad and envious eyes. Then, and just as Francesca is about to leave the room pushing a cartload of dirty pots, plates, glasses, and silverware, Yasmine remembers Esperanza.

"Senora Francesca,"

The Inn keeper stops and turns around, "Yes?"

"I was wondering if you have ever heard of a painting called Esperanza."

Francesca tilts her head questioningly, "Pardon?"

Yasmine takes a deep breath, leans forward, resting her elbows on the table, and explains, "I am looking for a mural called Esperanza. It is said to be covering a wall that faces the sea in a small fishing village…"

Francesca strikes a pensive pose, setting her right hand on her waist, elbow pointing slightly outward and back. Tapping with the sole of her black leather sandal rhythmically against the tiled floor, as if to summon some lost piece of memory, she frowns, eyes shifting from Yasmine, to the floor, to the wall, to the ceiling, before settling to her guest. The hostess nods, "Yes… Hmmm… Esperanza, you say? Hmmm… Yes, I have heard of it."

Yasmine's face lights up, "You heard of it."

"Yes, I did. At least twice, from guests who stopped here to stay for a night, just like you, and who inquired about the picture facing the sea, just like you."

"Do you know where it is?" Yasmine asks, with eyes transfixed on Francesca's lips.

"No," the hostess shakes her head, "The truth is I don't even know if it really exists. The guests who asked about this Esperanza never came back to let us know how their searches went." Then, and as if remembering something worth saying, she remarks, "But, it seems that you are on the right path... and that's always good to know."

Yasmine nods, trying to hide her disappointment, "It's better than nothing. Thank you, Francesca." Then standing up, she says, "I think it's time for me to go get some rest."

Francesca nods, wishing she could help some more, "Have a very good night, Senora."

"Good night, Francesca."

"Andalou, Did I ever tell you about my father?" Alberto finished lighting his last cigarette and flicked the smoking match in the glowing lamp post's direction. "My father, Nadal Aguilarez, a true warrior."

Andalou nodded, tucked his hands inside his coat pockets, and examined the empty street with a quick sweeping glance. He then turned to his old friend, inviting him with a hand gesture to start walking. It was a bright night, the kind of night that made Alberto remember and talk, and Andalou knew that all too well.

"My father, like all of his brothers, was born in a land torn between the love of its inhabitants and the greed of their neighbors. He heard the sound of guns, at too young an age."

A large roach appeared in front of them. Alberto watched it scurry around and between his feet, then Andalou's, in what seemed to be suicidal determination, before finally disappearing as it climbed down the curbside.

The gray haired sailor shook his head, "My father grew, too fast and too soon, to fight and struggle. He grew to face Franco's army, the way our people always faced their enemies, with courage and unflinching resolve."

Alberto paused, as if waiting for the sadness of remembrance to pass. Then, after a few steps, and a couple of deep breaths, he gazed up at the moon, perhaps not even noticing it, and resumed, "My father cried when he received news of Guarnica's bombing by German aircrafts, invited to intervene on behalf of Franco's government… a way as good as any other to test and demonstrate the devastating power of German aeronautical technology. And on that very day, my father swore that that son of a swine, Franco, and all of those who had come to his aid, supplying him with aircrafts, tanks and soldiers, would pay for the blood that was spilled, for the innocents that had been killed, children, women and men, harmless souls so cruelly disposed of...

"So by the time World War II started my father was already fighting, fighting his own war, not for a flag and not for a political party, but in the name of his people, for better days, for freedom and simply because there just was no other way to go about living. But quickly, his war and the bigger one got mixed up beyond distinction. So, he took sides, with the French, the British, and later the Americans, or perhaps it was them who actually joined him. But anyway, my father never lost sight of his reasons and aim. He fought with all of his heart, never worrying about his own life. And even his wounds, he carried with pride. Somehow, and no matter how much he had gone through, he still had faith in the future, faith in justice. He really believed that the end of the continental war would bring liberation to our people and to our land.

"Unfortunately, the Fates had different plans. Franco outlasted the war, and our beloved land remained under Spanish control. That is why my father, may the Good Lord bless his soul, kept on fighting, faithfully dreaming of an autonomous Basque land, an independent Basque country, where the Basque language would be heard, spoken and sung without any fear of repercussion."

In front of them, a black cat emerged from a dark alley. It mewed and with feline grace came to meet them. Andalou stopped and squatted to pet the friendly stray. He ran his fingers along its furry back as it purred and brushed against him.

When Andalou stood up, the cat, stretching its neck, moved toward Alberto who chuckled and said, "Sorry friend, we might smell like fish, but we don't have any food on us."

The cat mewed again and, swaying its tail in slow motion, watched them walk away, Alberto talking and Andalou listening.

"Let me tell you this. Nadal Aguilarez was a passionate man who inspired many. He stood at the forefront of every battle he participated in, be it through the labor movements that rose to put a stop to the bleeding of our land's resources and our people's talents and energies, or be it through the founding of ETA. Even after Franco's death, which disappointedly brought very little change, he continued to press for change and to challenge the oppressor."

Having reached the port's fence, they turned left and headed toward the lighted and guarded gate. Through a steel mesh fence, they could see, past the deserted docks, the locked warehouses and the hundreds of bulky containers, the ghostly shapes of resting ships.

Alberto slowed down and looked at his friend, "This was my father. This was his legacy. And this is why my brother and I followed in his footsteps, embracing his dreams, passions and aspirations, and ended up deeply involved with ETA, leading clandestine lives spent crossing the border that separates France from Spain, planning on one side and fighting on the other, the way many Basques, generation after generation, have had to do, in the name of freedom, in the name of everything we were born to be."

He spat and shook his head, "We knew the risks all

too well. After all, we had grown in a world where arrest and persecution were the norms. We saw our neighbors and friends disappear, to either never be seen again or to show up bruised and battered, days or weeks later, with horrifying tales of torture, beatings, and abuse by the Spanish police. Yes, we knew the risks... Actually, we were living at their edge, and so were our families."

At the gate, they showed their passports to the British guard and watched him examine their documents before handing them back and allowing them in. They thanked him and started toward their ship.

Alberto took a deep breath and sighed, "When they arrested my wife Maria, she was twenty-two years old and pregnant. Our baby was due in three months. I waited and prayed. I cried and prayed. They released her four days later. Her face was so bruised, she was hardly recognizable. She could barely eat and wouldn't speak for days. They had beaten her so hard that she suffered a miscarriage. And we were told that she would never be able to bear a child again..."

They were alone and surrounded by silence, concrete and steel. It was an indifferently cold and empty space, where Alberto couldn't stop remembering.

"Five months later, my father and my brother were sitting at a bar, talking and drinking, when three strangers walked in, pulled out automatic riffles from underneath their raincoats, and let hell break loose, killing both my brother and father, along with many other patrons who just happened to be there.

"That day," Alberto confided, "I cried and cursed our struggle and our enemy. I said, 'Enough is enough.' And, before the week was over, I climbed onto the back of a truck with Maria. I felt her fingernails digging into my hand. I looked at her. She smiled nervously, and I could see how frightened she was. I nodded and told her that everything will be alright. She lowered her head, trying to hide tears she could no longer hold. I could feel her pain. We sat silently and watched, as the rattling truck took us through and then away from streets I had known since I was child. I saw my town vanish in the darkness of cold night, and wondered how long our exile would last."

Driving through thick morning fog, not too far from Marbella, Yasmine cannot help feeling defeated. It is her fourth day on the road, and she is losing hope. She is so tempted to stop, yet she goes on, refusing to listen to that nagging inner voice that insists on berating her. She turns on the radio, hoping music would muffle her doubts. But the mocking words linger. They even get clearer, saying, "You fool… There is no village, no building, no wall, no painting to be found."

She curses herself, the radio, the road and the fog, as she hears her own pessimistic thought echoing within, "All of it is nothing but a dumb situation." She so is tired of driving, and blames Marbella's mad traffic for it. She swears at a truck because she feels that it is dangerously tailgating her. She is so tempted to stop, yet she forges on too stubborn to do so. She frowns apprehensively at the winding coastal road ahead of her, and wishes for a reason, an excuse, to take a break.

Five minutes later her wish is granted. A blurry sign appears in the distance, its lights weakly cutting through the fog, indicating the coming of some gas station. Squeezing the steering wheel with both hands, she presses her back into the seat she is tired of being on and, with a flick of a finger, switches on the car's right turn signals.

Once out of the car, she stretches by one of the gas pumps, fills her tank, goes inside the station to pay, grab a bottle of mineral water to drink, and ask the attendant about Esperanza, already guessing his answer.

"No Senora… never heard of it. Sorry," the man behind the counter, as expected, shakes his head in the negative.

Yasmine thanks him, while pocketing her change,

when an old man, who instead of standing in line behind her, steps forward, and so close to her that she has to move aside.

The old man, clutching the counter, nods at the attendant and asks with a rusty voice, "Sebastian, can you hand me a pack of those," pointing to some local brand of cigarettes, "and some matches?"

Yasmine braces herself to shoot him an irritated and-how-about-waiting-for-your-turn sort of look, but as he turns toward her, she softens, surprised by the warmth she glimpses in his eyes.

He smiles, wrinkling a coarse looking face burnt by the sun, "Forgive me Senora, I did not mean to rush you." He lowers his head as if to express remorse, "It is just that at my age, my legs refuse to hold me up for too long."

"No, no, it's not a problem..." she waves her hand, "I was on my way out anyway." Then having offered a conciliatory nod, she starts walking toward the door.

"Senora," the word brings her to a halt.

She turns to look at the old stranger with a puzzled face, "Yes?"

"Would you mind giving me a ride back? I live on this road, less than five hundred meters from here."

Hesitant, Yasmine glances helplessly at the attendant who, preferring not to get involved in the exchange, makes an effort at appearing busy tinkering with the register. She looks back at the old man, wanting to say no, him being a stranger, and her being a traveling woman on her own. But, as she sets her eyes on his frail frame, she recognizes a new impression, quieting and reassuring, arising within. Quickly, the impression germinates into a thought saying, "There is nothing to fear. This old fellow is hardly able to stand." So, choosing to trust her intuition, between a nod and another, she says, "Why not? Five hundred meters isn't that far, after all."

The elder pays for his cigarettes and follows her to the car.

She opens the passenger door for him, holds his arm as he struggles to get in. Having closed his door, she walks around the vehicle, gets in, fastens her seat belt and, with a patient smile, asks him, "Which way, Senor?"

"That way," he raises a hand and, with an extended index, points to the left.

Yasmine starts the engine. The old man straightens his back, stiffening from the eyebrows down, as if he were in a jet that is about to take off, and holds on tightly to the seat, as the car begins moving forward, until, reaching the road, and slowly turning left, leaves gravel and dirt behind –traveling in the opposite direction Yasmine was initially heading.

"So, you're looking for Esperanza?" the old man asks while keeping his eyes intently fixated on the road.

Yasmine shifts to fourth gear and glances at him, looking a bit startled, "Yes, do you know where I can find it?"

"It's about half an hour from my house, if you keep on going this way."

Unable to believe her ears, she protests, "… but I came from that direction, and I didn't see any village in the past half hour. Are you sure…"

He interrupts her, "Of course I'm sure. My brother lives there. The village is very small, hidden behind some shrubbery and some trees, and whatnot, very easy to miss, especially with this fog… Oh, you can drop me here."

She slows the car down, bringing it to a stop on the side of the road, and asks him before he opens his door, "Are there any markers I should be looking for?"

"A marker…" he scratches his bolding freckled head, "N-no, I can't think of one. Actually, there is the dirt road that cuts through the trees. Look for that. It leads there." He opens the door and sets one foot out. But just as he is about to stand, he lifts the left sleeve of his jacket, revealing an antique looking wrist watch and, squinting with great focus, checks the time, "I am afraid You might not be able to find the dirt road." He glances at Yasmine, who hasn't taken her eyes off of him since they stopped, "If you would like, I can show you where the village is. I haven't seen my brother for at least a month now; this would be a good excuse to pay the old fart a visit."

Disliking the idea of driving off of the main road, behind trees, with a stranger, Yasmine wants to say no, because, frankly, it seems, to her better judgment, rather unwise. Yet, with part of her strongly believing that there isn't any other alternative, she accepts his offer, hoping for the best, and hears herself say, "That would be wonderful. Thank you."

But as soon as the old man settles back on the passenger seat and closes the door, doubt, in a split second, creeps back into her mind and leads her to reassess the whole deal. She looks at him again, a many murder stories documented on TV coming to mind, and asks suspiciously, "How come the attendant at the gas station didn't know about it?"

The man chuckles, "Sebastian has not lived here for very long," he waves his hand dismissively, "Plus, not too many people know about Esperanza, or as some like to call her, the priestess of hope." He pauses while looking at her, "They say that only those with broken hearts and lost dreams know and seek her."

Yasmine, aware that his eyes are set on her, keeps hers on the road, no longer capable of choosing between trust and fear, "What else can you tell me about this mural?"

The old passenger scratches his beardless chin, "Well… It all started a few years ago, when an unknown sailor arrived to my brother's village, and if my brother was telling you this he would say that the sailor had come accompanied with the northern winds. But, anyway, my brother being a certified ass, please excuse my language…"

Yasmine smiles, relaxing a bit.

"I'm not lying and you can ask anyone who knows him. They'll tell you… But I'm digressing. Please forgive me. Damn old age makes me babble in circles. And by the way, where was I? Oh yes… So apparently this stranger, whom no one had been expecting to see, arrived and settled in my brother's village to fulfill a promise he had made. The promise was one he had made, while at sea, to a sailor who was actually from the village."

The old man reaches into his jacket's pocket, pulls out the sealed box of cigarettes he's just purchased, and, looking at the driver, asks, "Do you mind if…?"

Yasmine replies with a wave of the hand, "Go ahead."

Shakily, and after a few grunts, he tears open the plastic wrap, "As I said, This new comer had promised his friend that he would move to the village, take care of the deceased's wife and son and build a woodshop on the beach. And listen to this, for here comes the strangest part, he promised his friend to cover one of the woodshop's walls, and not any wall, no, he specifically promised to cover the wall that is facing the sea with a painting inspired from the heart. "

Pausing, he strikes a match, and, using both hands to protect the generated flame, lights the cigarette hanging between his lips. For a few seconds, his sunken cheeks sink further in, as he fills his lungs with nicotine. Then, and slowly, his face regains its normal shape as he blows smoke out of his nostrils and speaks again, "A year passed and the shop was built. The widow and her son were taken care of."

The tip of his cigarette glows to a brighter red, "Yet, there was no picture, apparently Andalou... Did I mention that his name was Andalou? Yes, Andalou… anyway, he had problems deciding what to paint." The old man presses on the window control switch on his door bringing the passenger window down, just enough to have the ashes of his burning cigarette blown out, "Or so it appeared, until one day, some two years ago, if I recall correctly, but then again… at my age, the memories of years past to blend into each other."

Pausing, he closes the window, then continues, "…until one day, the villagers awoke and found the completed picture of a beautiful woman, wearing a beautiful light, white dress that appears in perpetual movement, as it were blown and lifted by the..."

Suddenly, He stops talking and, slowly, turns his head to look at the driver.

Yasmine gazes at him quickly, and finds him staring at her with an opened mouth and bulging eyes, as if he were chocking, "Are you alright?"

He coughs, "Ex-cuse me," he stutters, "I-I'm fine,

thank you." He straightens himself on his seat, "Just my mind playing tricks on me, at my age it's nothing to worry about," he glances at her again and starts shaking his head. Then, noticing that Yasmine's posture has stiffened and that the car is slowing down, he blushes embarrassedly and starts drawing smoke into his lungs, before allowing it to escape through his nostrils a few seconds later.

"And, what was I saying again? Oh, yes, I remember," he chuckles, "so the villagers woke up, and where they had left the most regular looking white wall the previous evening, they found the stirring image of a young woman standing with both arms extended, palms opened, with a butterfly suspended in midair above one of them, along with both Andalou and the widow standing in front of her and weeping." The old man laughs, "And thus was born the mural you are looking for."

"Esperanza?"

"Yes, Esperanza. The priestess of hope," the old man nods. "But as far as the name Esperanza goes, it wasn't given until a few weeks after its appearance, with the widow, lying sick in bed, and, in fact, about to die, or as the villagers prefer describing her state, on her way to join the man she loved… Anyway, it was right there, on her death bed, that she herself requested that the mural be named Esperanza."

He looks at Yasmine and smiles, glad to see her posture relaxing, "Now, ever since the widow died, many unusual things began happening. Strangers began showing up from all around the world, from distant countries, some of which we, here, had never heard of. They started coming, looking for a painting that, from what we heard them say, appeared in their dreams, or was revealed to them by someone who had vaguely heard about it. They come, just like you, to meet Esperanza." Shaking his head, he asks, "Isn't that something now?"

"Since I started looking for this mural, I asked so many people and looked in so many books. Nobody knows anything about it. There not a single word written about it. It is as if it doesn't really exist..." Yasmine slows the car down, as they approach a snaking section of the road.

The old man nods, "Yet, you're looking for it...

"Yes, I am; despite my best judgment, despite all the confused looks I've been given about this painting that is apparently so fantastic people should have heard about it."

"Well, most people are Catholic here. Our faith doesn't really approve of priestesses... In fact, it admonishes them. Anyway, the thing is, you see, had Andalou agreed to change the name to a less blasphemous one, the way the local clergy had suggested, the mural would have been on every television channel... and I mean all around the world. Unfortunately, he refused, you know... to keep the word he'd given the widow, that is. Unable to compromise, Andalou left the church no other option, but to admonish the wall and declare it sacrilegious... Oh, there is the road I told you about."

Yasmine leans forward, squinting and searching through the misty fog. "I see it!" she exclaims, sounding exhilarated, "And you were absolutely right. I would have never been found it on my own."

Slowing down, she turns into a small dirt path shyly hiding between bushes and trees. She swallows nervously as her tires meet the unpaved road and flood the car with a myriad of new sounds, from broken leaves and branches, pebbles unearthed and mud compressed. Twice, the whole vehicle tilts to one side and then to the other, jerking both passengers uncomfortably. Yasmine slows down some more, and holds firmly onto the steering wheel, to keep her body from bouncing and rocking.

The old man stops talking and braces himself by pressing his hands against the dashboard. Yasmine, about to ask him how long they would have to go before reaching the village, bounces on her seat as the first houses appear to her, white and ghostly, their simple shapes barely escaping the thick morning haze.

Slowly, the houses gain solidity, grow in size and multiply. They become palpable, as closeness extricates them from the shrouding mist, so that when Yasmine passes them, she has no problem discerning the bright colors of some doors, the shape of potted plants sitting on window sills, simple tools leaning against whitewashed walls, and people, slowly walking, or just standing frozen, as if caught by surprise by the sudden apparition of unannounced visitors.

The old man points, "There is my brother's home. Could you drop me here?"

"Of course," Yasmine gets as close as she can to the

house belonging to her guide's sibling, shifts to neutral, parks the car and turns off the engine.

The old man unbuckles his seatbelt with great relief, "The mural is on the last building, at the end of the road. You can leave your car here and continue on foot. It isn't very far. It will be better that way; the road gets worse as it nears the beach."

She thanks him, once they both get out of the car. Wishing her good luck, the old man departs making for the house. For a moment, Yasmine watches him wobble away, then, turning around, faces the road and takes a deep breath. Engulfed in foggy silence, she tries to summon as much strength and courage as can be found within. Then after waiting a few seconds, she steps forward, unclear about what to expect, willing to follow hope and conclude this mad journey she has somehow embarked on, whatever the outcome, whatever the ending.

A soft westerly breeze was blowing when the old stranger joined Andalou, who was staring at a wall of a plain building standing at the edge of a sandy beach. He said, "Hello," and smiled when Andalou looked at him.

"Oh, I'm sorry, I didn't see you coming. How can I help you?"

"I was hoping you could direct me to the closest water fountain or spring," he smiled and added, "I need to fill my water gourd."

"Water fountain…" Andalou scratched the back of his neck and said, "You can come to my home, there is water there."

"Thank you very much, Senor," the man's wrinkled face lit up.

"I don't live very far," said Andalou, inviting the stranger to follow him with his opened palm, before adding, "My name is Andalou."

"Paulo Aduro, at your service," nodded the old man, shaking Andalou's hand.

"And what brings you into our village, Senor Aduro?"

"An old friend of mine used to live here," replied Paulo with a smile.

Andalou nodded and directed his guest past the large building, "…used to?"

"He died some fifteen years ago… and, by the way, his shed was right where I found you standing."

"Really?" Andalou glanced quickly at the back of his shop, "You must be talking about the man the villagers refer to as El-Viejo. I was told that he was the one who owned this land years ago."

"hmm... I think you're right. El-Viejo, that's what they called him..."

"And, you were a friend of his... From what I heard, he was quite a reserved character."

"I would say that he was a man of very few words. Some men are like that, born to accomplish and act, reverent in silent quietude, not inclined to partake in pointless rhetoric."

"It sounds like you have a lot of respect for him," remarked Andalou.

"I definitely do. He was a friend, a good friend."

Andalou nodded, remembering his old friend Alberto,

Paulo shook his head, "And an impressive man with that too."

"You know, now I remember a neighbor telling me a story about him sailing into the heart of a storm to bring back three children that had gone fishing in a small bark and hadn't returned. Is that true?"

"It is, and it is actually because of that immense display of courage that he was accepted into the village and offered the piece of land in front of the beach, as a gift from the locals."

"I didn't know that he wasn't a local..." said Andalou.

"El-Viejo, as they call him, was definitely not a local," confirmed Paulo, "He had arrived to this area a long time ago, to be more precise, just a few months after General Franco died, and Juan Carlos was crowned king, not that these events, or any political change that affected the country mattered that much on this beach, but from what he'd told me, they did to him.

"Anyway, El-Viejo, before he was known as such, pitched a tent in front of the sea, at the edge of this beach, right behind those shrubs and trees that stretch along the beach and the forest. He started living there, unseen and unheard. He built himself a raft, and subsisted on whatever he could catch.

"For more than a year, the villagers didn't even notice his presence. His tent was practically invisible, concealed behind a thick wall of bushes. There were talks about, a small boat that was seen in the water during a couple of full moon nights. At first, the story was taken with a heavy dose of skepticism. In fact, it was even considered dubious, especially since its source was a man known for his affliction with an great affinity for the bottle. But, then, as more people saw the supposed 'ghost boat,' apologies, along with compensation in the form of liquefied and bottled alcoholic nectar, were made to the poor mocked witness."

Paulo chuckled and then sighed at what he liked calling 'the sweet ironies of life.' He looked at his host, found him enthralled in the story, and went on, "Yet, it wasn't until months later, and only because he saved the three boys, that the villagers found out about their new neighbor, and decided after much talk, that such a brave man shouldn't be living in a tent. So, they offered him some land, welcomed him into their small community, and called him El-Viejo."

Andalou nodded, reminded of his own story, carried by Alberto's letter, caught in Maria's tears, shaken by Caesar's eyes, and finally accepted and embraced by the village.

"The building looks fairly new," remarked Paulo,

pointing to the large structure in front of which they had met, "I don't recall it being there the last time I visited this place. Although, I have to admit, a long time has passed since then."

"It is new," agreed Andalou, explaining, "I finished building it about a year ago."

Paulo gazed at Andalou, "You built it?"

"Brick by brick," answered Andalou.

"That is impressive, Senor. It must have taken a lot of time and energy."

Andalou nodded and, rubbing the back of his neck, added, "And it's not even finished."

"It isn't?" asked Paulo surprised.

"Not really..." confirmed Andalou, shaking his head, "I still have to paint the back wall."

"Oh, that shouldn't take you very long... A couple of coats and you're done. If you'd like I can give you a hand."

Andalou smiled, "I wish it were that easy, Senor... but thank you for the offer."

Curling his lips, Paulo tilted his head and said, "I have to admit that I am having difficulty understanding, Senor."

Andalou shook his head, "I'm supposed to paint something artistic on this wall..."

"Oh, I see..." nodded Paulo with a raised eyebrow, "and, I have to rescind my offer, for I surely lack the kind of artistic talent the task you are faced with requires."

Andalou chuckled and said, "I totally understand, Senor Aduro. I totally understand."

Upon arriving at the entrance of a modest white house, in front of which a few hens and a rooster were pecking at the ground, Andalou knocked at the door -as tradition required from men about to enter any home inhabited by a woman.

"Come in," said a warm-sounding feminine voice from inside the house.

Andalou opened the door and announced, "Maria, I'm bringing company."

The voice replied, "Excellent, lunch is almost ready."

Andalou stepped aside and gestured for his guest to walk in first. Paulo smiled, set his right hand on the house's stucco façade and closed his eyes, while a silent prayer filled his heart. Then, stepping in with his right foot first, he entered.

Andalou followed him, closed the door, and asked, "Would you be interested in joining us for lunch?"

Paulo grinned, "Senor Andalou, I never refuse an invitation to share a meal…" He chuckled and added, "Plus, I have to confess that I am quite hungry."

Andalou laughed jovially, "That is perfect. Maria, as you will soon discover, has a tendency to cook for a whole regiment."

"That is a sign of great generosity," commented Paulo.

"Thank you, Senor." Maria had just walked out of the kitchen to greet the announced guest.

Paulo bowed, "If anyone deserves to be thanked it is definitely you Senora."

Maria stepped forward.

"Senor Aduro, allow me to introduce you to our host, Maria Vantisso."

Paulo took a deep inhalation and said, "Senora Vantisso, my name is Paulo Aduro. And I am mostly honored to meet you."

Maria smiled, shook the visitor's hand and said, "You can call me Maria."

Paulo bowed again, "And you can call me Paulo." He gently took her hand in his, and brought it to his lips.

Pleasantly surprised, Maria glanced at Andalou who was grinning, and said, "Well... come on in, Paulo."

Paulo nodded and followed Maria, from the corridor to the living room, where he was offered a seat on one of the many wooden chairs surrounding a very old wooden rectangular table. He put aside the traveling bag that was slung over his left shoulder and sat down.

Maria asked, "What would you like to drink? We have wine, tea, water, and some carbonated orange beverages."

"A glass of water would be great."

"...and how about you, Andalou?"

Andalou waved a hand, "Please, Maria, relax, take your seat. I'll get the drinks. What would you like?"

"I'll have a Fanta. Thank you."

Andalou nodded and headed for the kitchen, but as he was about to reach the door he turned around and said, "And, guess what Maria, Senor Aduro told me that he was a friend of El-Viejo."

Maria glanced at Paulo and asked, "...the same El-Viejo who used to own the land in front of the beach?"

"Yes, Senora," confirmed Paulo with a smile.

"And what did I say about Senora," complained Maria with a raise brow and a grin on her face.

"Forgive me, Maria... old habits are hard to change, but, I'll work on it."

"Good," said Maria, with a giggle.

Andalou laughed and disappeared into the kitchen.

"I heard so many things about that man," confessed Maria, "Is it true that he couldn't speak?"

"Not exactly," replied Paulo, "he actually refused to talk, unless it was necessary."

"Are you sure? I heard from many that no one had ever heard him say a word…"

"You can believe me, Se…" Paulo chuckled, "Maria. He could speak."

Maria nodded, a questioning expression marking her face, and asked, "I was told that he was much of a recluse… May I ask you how you came to know him?"

"Of course, I met him, on the road, on his way back home, and ended up traveling with him, all the way from Tarifa, until arriving here."

"…home?" questioned Maria, "but, he wasn't from here."

"You're right. He was from a mountainous area on the other side of the Mediterranean. He actually told me, while standing at the beach and pointing to the horizon that his native village was exactly across the sea from us."

"Why did he stay here, then? Why didn't he go back?"

"I asked him the same question," replied Paulo.

Highly interested, Maria leaned forward and inquired, "Did he tell you why?"

"He did. He said that he couldn't. He wanted to, but he simply couldn't. He said that he had lost too much, that there was too much pain awaiting his return. He said that standing on this beach was good enough."

Maria thought of herself and remembered how painful loss could be. Feeling closeness to the image of a man who could not cross the sea and face his past, she asked, "What was his name?"

"Jazil. His name was Jazil."

Maria repeated the dead man's name, feeling it inside her mouth, inside her head, and nodded, as if reverently. Her eyes wandered for a moment, into a corner of the living room, as she asked, "So, is it his memory that brings you back here?"

"In a way, Maria, in a way. Personally, I like to believe that the wind has something to do with it," he smiled.

"The wind?" repeated Maria, surprised by his unexpected reply, "I guess that there is no way to find out where you'll end up, then."

"Wherever it is, I am sure that it will be just fine."

When Andalou walked back into the room, carrying a tray of iced beverages, he was greeted back with grins from both Maria and Paulo.

Then, Maria asked, "Did you know that our guest is a wind follower?"

Andalou glanced at Paulo, with a puzzled face and said, "Is this true?"

Paulo nodded, "In a way…"

"That must be a very exciting way of living," noted Andalou.

Paulo's eyes sparked with interest, "Only someone who has wandered for a while would say that."

Andalou nodded.

Maria laughed gingerly, "I bet you two have a lot in common."

That day, charmed by Paulo's personality, Andalou and Maria relaxed and opened their hearts. They sat and allowed themselves to be lead by the sweetness of their guest's voice, as he talked about life, love and traveling, sharing tales meant to completely discard any limitation set by mankind, while stretching over a boundless and unified planet, going beyond the separation that is created with every drawn boundary, the isolation that afflicts nationalities, and challenging the very prevailing notion of proprietorship. They listened to him speak and drifted with the openness, and limitlessness of possibilities implied in his stories and ideas.

When lunch time came, Andalou and Maria sat up the table, insisting that Paulo relax anytime he offered to help them. Then, they had a warm and spiced meal of roasted fish and fried tomatoes. Taking their time and enjoying the sweetness of the moment, they shared a bottle of wine, along stories about far away places, about lost ones, and, about hope.

Paulo learned about little Carlos's birth –finding it miraculous. He listened, smiling as Maria described proudly how intelligent, helpful and caring her son was. He nodded, offering a consoling gaze to the widow, as he found out about Alberto's death. He sighed, understandingly, when she talked about Andalou, about promises made and kept. He was moved listening to Maria, as she told him about her life, love, struggle, torture, loss, her being told that she would never be able to give birth, escaping the evil of those in power, sacrifice, and hiding from the past. He saw pain in her eyes, and offered compassion through his.

Paulo listened to Andalou conceal his past behind

openly chosen and revealed truths, as he shared stories about his days as a smuggler in the Mediterranean, recalling his direst years, those he spent in the company of cold uncertainty, living in the shadows, thriving on danger and closeness to death, until Alberto found him. Alberto was his brother, his teacher, his savior, the man who got him out of darkness and restored hope in his heart. Paulo saw regret in his generous host's irises and offered a soft smile, a token of better days to come.

Then, on his way out, Paulo looked at Maria and told her that love was boundless, beyond death and life. He looked at Andalou and told him that sometimes it is better to accept than deny, for what one rejects is what one begets. He told him, "Your past is in you, as well as your future. They are both in your heart." He told him, "…as long as you keep your heart muffled the wall shall remain a blank canvas." He shook Andalou's hand and advised, "Look within, son. Unveil the truth. Set it free. Let it move you. Let it find your hands. Then, hold brush and paint, and face that white wall. Your heart shall guide you." Wind blew from the east, brushing alongside the house. Paulo wished them good-bye and was soon heading west.

Yasmine forges in, one step at a time, one breath at a time, ignoring the way those she passes stare at her, their whispers, as well as the sign of the cross they make with their hands, until, she finally hears the sea's hushed call. Then, and all of the sudden, under her feet, dirt and grass give way to softer sand, and all around her, the fog begins dissolving. It all happens so quickly that Yasmine wonders if she isn't dreaming the whole thing.

She slows down, hesitating, afraid of what she might find, struggling to accept the strangeness that permeates the unfamiliar surroundings she has walked into, for everything seems shrouded with eeriness, even the few boats resting capsized, guarded by a flock of seagulls, that emerge to meet her, right as she passes a large building trapped in sand.

She is so close to her goal that her whole being -mind and body, heart and guts, every cell and fiber that makes her- is pulled onward in time and space toward a culminating point where a story told and reality cross paths, for better or worst. Her heart is pounding. Her legs are shaking. Her senses are overwhelmed with fears too irrational to be argued away. Yet, she pushes through because turning around is absolutely out of the question.

Her feet sink into the formless sand, until they are submerged to the ankles, forcing her to press on harder, her eyes locked on the building's corner around which the mural should be. Her pulse is getting faster, almost out of control, but it doesn't matter, because the corner is at arm's reach. The fog is all gone, as if it never had been. The sky, the sea and the beach are all clear, blue over gold. Seagulls are seagulls and boats are boats. Suddenly, she realizes that if she stood between the boats and the mural she would be able to see the picture in its entirety. So she starts sprinting toward the boats and the seagulls, refusing to look at Esperanza yet.

Breathless, Yasmine stops and spins on her heels, to find that a throng of people, gathered by the building she just passed, are watching her. Her eyes blur them out. In fact everything, besides the character captured on the wall, becomes part of unimportant details that are given no other option but to be pressed into a mostly irrelevant background, as Yasmine comes face to face with Esperanza.

By the boats, Yasmine stands still, unable to move, lost in the silence of a blank mind, her ability to formulate ideas deconstructed, chattered and blown away by what, or to be more accurate whom, she sees in front of her. She stands there, as empty and shallow as emptiness itself, until her brain, as if having somehow rewired itself back into life, finds a way to slip away into a more palpable consciousness, from which it is able to pull the bright individual Yasmine is out of a deep dreamy nothingness and into the now and here, a place real enough for her nervous system to function properly, a space where she is allowed to process what her eyes are seeing.

She blinks, once, twice, and suddenly, realizes who she is staring at. And, when she does, her lower jaw drops open, but no words come out.

Slowly, she begins moving toward the mural, watching it expand with every step taken, swallowing all matter around it, a black hole no grain of rationality can escape. Until, Esperanza lets go, and the world reappears. Yasmine, ten meters away from the wall, stops to study the priestess of hope now facing her.

She can hear whispers coming from the crowd, "It's

her…" She can hear them arguing, "How could that be?" They sound excited, "It's a miracle." She can hear what she is incapable of shouting, "It's her. It's Esperanza."

She turns to them, scanning each and every face in search of an explanation. Unfortunately they're all as bewildered as she is. She takes a deep breath, looks at the woman on the wall, and, ignoring the tightness gnawing at her stomach, starts walking toward the spectators.

Yasmine had thought of this moment in many occasions, trying to imagine what Esperanza would look like. She had pictured herself standing, in front of the mural, with tears running down her face. She had imagined a situation that would bring out all the hidden feelings and emotions that poison her days, so that they may be flushed out of her body and mind. She had foreseen an encounter that would set her heart free, and liberate her once and for all, from the all pain and sorrow she has been living in. Yet, never had she expected that Esperanza would look exactly the way she does, or more precisely, did a few years ago.

The villagers watch the living image of their Esperanza walk their way. Unable to take their eyes of her, they stare in silence, with perhaps a mixture of astonishment, disbelief and awe distorting their frozen expressions.

Yasmine stops in front of them, her body shaking, "Where can I find the man who painted this wall?"

An elderly woman, standing to her left, speaks, while the others remain still, save furtive evocations of the holy trinity with quick hand gestures. "He lives and works in the shop," she points to the building on which the mural is painted.

"Thank you," replies Yasmine, before excusing herself, as she cuts through the stomped gathering, and heads for the only door she can see.

The green door feels and sounds solid, as Yasmine knocks on it. She waits for an answer, but there is no answer to be heard. She tries again, this time, hitting the door much harder with the palm of her right hand. She looks behind her, to see if the villagers are still there —and they are. She hears a clicking noise, probably the unlatching of a lock. Yasmine steps back, and watches the door as it opens with a squeak, revealing a boy – a boy she has seen before. She brings her hand to her mouth, and holds herself from screaming; it is the child from her dreams. Carlos freezes; he too recognizes Esperanza. The crowd moves closer forming half a circle, around Yasmine, as if to keep her from running away.

"…Esperanza?" Carlos sets a foot out, "You're Esperanza, right?"

Yasmine laughs nervously, "No." She shifts on her feet uncomfortably, "At least I don't think I am," and managing to smile, she asks, "What is your name?"

"Carlos," he glances behind him, into the hallway he is standing in, as if to check if someone is there.

She repeats his name, "Carlos," and smiles appreciatively, "My name is Yasmine."

Carlos's chest rises and collapses anxiously, but no word escapes his lips.

Yasmine steps forward, moving very slowly, so as not to frighten him, "Is the man who painted Esperanza here?"

Carlos shifts slightly, "Uncle Andalou is in the back. He is working."

Interlacing her fingers, her hands tightly held together, Yasmine pleads, "Would you mind taking me to him?"

Staring at the crowd encircling Yasmine, the boy nods,

"C-come with me." Then, moving aside, he holds the door opened for Esperanza's living replica to enter.

"Thank you," Yasmine smiles, before walking through the door, and disappearing at once from the crowd's sight, as Carlos shuts the door behind her.

Carlos slides past the unexpected visitor, "The work area is in the back." He starts walking, turns around finds her still standing by the door, staring at him as if he were a ghost. He smiles nervously, "It's this way."

Yasmine nods, unblinking, and stats following, she has not a shadow of a doubt, the boy from her dreams.

They enter a modestly decorated living room, brightly lit by sunlight entering from a large window facing a wall on which are hanging two framed paintings —one of a sailboat cruising through blue open water, the other of a white light house standing on the edge of a rocky cliff on which a foamy wave is suspended in mid-bursting.

Yasmine recognizing the light house stops, her mouth opened in incomprehension.

Carlos opens another door, walks into another room, and calls, "Senora! This way, senora."

Startled, she swallows dry nervousness, and heads for the door, her eyes still transfixed on the painting.

Past the door, stepping on a floor covered with a thick layer of saw dust, she walks underneath a loft, extending over almost half of the room. She quickly passes row upon row of stacked up wood logs, all perfectly sorted by size, as well as by shape, trying to keep up with the boy who is too excited to slow down, as he leads her through yet another room -one where space is divided into two sections, one containing tables, bed frames, chairs, dressers, and chests, while the other is filled with two large work benches supporting different types of saws, and a great variety of tools hanging on the wall.

"This way," calls Carlos, as he turns into a dark corner and disappears behind a gray shelf.

Yasmine follows her guide's voice, as his silhouette blends with the shadows before reemerging, just as he pushes a door open, flooding the corridor they're both in with blinding light. She raises her right hand, bringing it in front of her face and squints, moving her head from side to side, trying to see past the door. As her vision begins adjusting to the light, she discerns the vague silhouette of a man, standing in the very far end of the brightly lit room.

She takes a step forward, noticing that the standing figure is facing a large canvas, and holding a thin paint brush in one of his hands. Her eyes slide along the painter's hand, arm, shoulder and neck to find the sharpened feature of his face. She stops walking and leans on the door frame. Andalou turns his head to the door. Their eyes meet, for less than a second, but that is enough; they recognize one another.

Stunned, Andalou lets the brush slip from his fingers and fall on the floor. He watches as Yasmine flees, disappearing behind Carlos who, with apprehensively unblinking eyes, stares at the red stroke the brush has made on the floor. Wobbling his way out of the room, Andalou passes Carlos, trips at the door, narrowly avoids falling, and runs through the building to catch Yasmine. He sprints past the crowd gathered next to his home, in the direction they're facing, toward the beach, behind his shop. He turns at the building's corner, sees her and slows down.

It had been less than a week since the northwestern winds had been replaced by a warmer southeasterly, when Paulo crossed Nasr street, maneuvering his way around two teenagers who were busy varnishing a wide round table propped by the entrance of a shop where a man, bent at the waist, was carving a winding pattern with a thin chisel on a panel clamped to a thickly built work bench. The old traveler stopped, his eyes caught by the unbroken motion of the sharp-edged tool, and the precise movements of a master's steady hand.

Slowly, he stepped into the shop, a wide square of a room filled with large cutting machines, hand tools and wood panels stacked on rakes standing against the wall directly to his left. He cleared his throat to let the absorbed worker know about his presence.

The artisan lifted his head and greeted the old visitor with a sweating forehead, a proud smile, and a warm, "Asalam alaykoom."

Paulo smiled back and replied, "Wa alaykoom asalam."

"What can I do for you, brother?" asked the thickly built, dark-haired wood carver.

"I was just walking by when I saw you working and decided to take a look at what you're making."

"Hmm… Well, come on in, then." He touched the panel he was reshaping, "I'm almost done with this one. It's a sideboard for a traditional sofa, and when it is ready, it will look just like that one over there, the one to your right."

Paulo looked to his right and found leaning against the wall a vibrantly varnished panel on which ran, lengthwise, and from one end to the other, beautiful carvings of mostly elongated and intertwining arabesques, wavy leaves and five petal flowers. Moving closer to the panel, he said, "This is truly beautiful… there is such precision in the details."

"Thank you. My name is Khaled," the artisan extended a hand, appreciating the compliment.

"Paulo. Pleasure making your acquaintance," the traveler clasped the shop's owner's hand, before asking, "How long have you been doing this kind of work?"

Khaled waved a suggestive hand, "Oh, I started when I was twelve years old."

Paulo nodded, "Following the in footsteps of your father, I venture."

Khaled shook his head, "No, my father was a civil servant, and if it had been up to him I would be doing something completely different."

"Watching you work, I can see that you have made a wise career choice."

The artisan laughed, "More of a calling, and all out of God's benevolence."

The old man smiled, "Rarely, do I meet men satisfied with their work."

"I praise Him everyday for everything. For hadn't I taken the path that led me here, I don't know where I'd be now. You see, at age twelve I wasn't doing too well at school. Already, I preferred spending time in the neighborhood's woodshop, helping around the best I can, and also, and most importantly, watching the master carver at work. Then, one day, the master carver came to my house and asked to see my father. My father welcomed the master carver and invited him to have some tea in the living room. An hour or so later, my father called me and asked me to sit down.

"My father said, 'Haj Ali thinks that you have a natural talent for working with wood. He knows that you're having problems at school and has offered to make you his apprentice. Before you answer, I want you to think about this very carefully. We'll have to get you out of school. You'll need to commit to working, very hard, every day. You'll have to listen to Haj Ali, do as he says, if you want to become a good wood carver, which is the only career option you'll have if you decide to quit school and become the Haj's apprentice. You don't have to give us an answer now. Go and think about it. Sit on the idea for a day or two, then come back and let me know.' I stood up, nodded at my father, shook Haj Ali's hand, and left the room, struggling to contain my excitement from taking hold of me, and already certain of my answer."

Paulo nodded, "Your father must be proud of you."

"He is now, but in the beginning, of course, he wasn't too keen about the decision I'd made. He would have loved seeing me become a doctor or a lawyer, or an engineer, but he never interfered. He let me follow my own path and supported me until I became self-reliant," Khaled shook his head and added, with a sincere sounding voice, "I don't know why I'm telling you all this…"

"We all need to talk at times…" Paulo stopped midsentence and tilted his head, looking, with great interest past Khaled, "Did you make those?"

The wood carver turned around to confirm his suspicion that what his unexpected visitor was referring to was actually a shelve on which were standing a few little wooden objects, small replicas of a tree, a mosque, a sailing ship, Fatima's protective hand, and a football. Then, just to clarify, he asked, "You mean the pieces on the shelf?"

"Yes, those," nodded Paulo.

"Yes. I made them during my very first years of apprenticeship," Khaled rubbed the back of his neck, adding in a rather amused tone, "In fact, I almost forgot they were there."

Paulo headed toward the shelf and inquired, "Would you mind if I took a look?"

"Not at all, go ahead, but just to let you know they're not for sale."

The old visitor reached up and grabbed one of the objects, turned it very slowly between his fingers, seriously examining its details. He looked at the artisan and smiled with a raised eyebrow. He opened his month to say something, but was interrupted by a loud "A salamo alaykoom!" Three men had entered the shop like a strong unsettling gust of wind, hands gesticulating, arms swaying in great flourishes, and were marching toward the wood carver.

Khaled nodded in Paulo's direction to excuse himself and turned to greet the trio, who had probably come to do business, their heads full of ideas they were eager to see represented on paper.

Paulo sat the ball back on the shelf, thanked his host, saluted the highly expressive trio, and walked out of the shop. Outside, he stopped by the helpers, started talking to them, while taking off his battered traveling bag, digging into it and pulling an object he handed to one of the teenagers, in an exchange Khaled didn't miss. Then,

Paulo, having thanked the young workers, slung his bag over his shoulders and took off.

One hour and forty-two minutes later, the three animated men, accompanied by Khaled, walked out of the store, in the same manner they had entered, still gesticulating, but rather satisfied by the deal made, and by what was accomplished as a result of the tenuous bargaining they had participated in. They shook hands and left, still debating their irreconcilable artistic preferences, yet looking more in agreement as when they first appeared.

Abd Ana-eem called his boss, "M-alem —teacher, the old man who was here earlier left you this." He pulled out of his pocket a round spherical object the size of a plum, a football carved out of wood, and handed it to his boss.

Khaled reached for the ball, gazed over his shoulder and inside his shop, thinking that it was rather bizarre for the old stranger to take the piece from the shelf it had been sitting on for years, just to hand it to Abd An-eem instead of simply setting it back where it belonged. Then, just as he is about to make a comment on what he believed had occurred, his eyes caught sight of a piece identical to the one he was holding sitting on the shelf. He closed his eyes and opened them again. The ball was definitely on the shelf.

With a confused look on his face, he turned to his apprentice and asked, "What is this?"

Abd Ana-eem shrugged his shoulders, opened his month to state the obvious, but then remembered something, "The man wanted me to tell you that he found it in his bag after staying in a small village in Spain, in Andalusia, on the coast… oh, yes, he also said that he had met a carpenter, a very generous man, and… he thinks it might have belonged to him."

Khaled stared back at the ball he was holding in his

hand, and noticed a detail that made his eyes bulge out in shock. He blinked once, twice, but the etching didn't disappear. It remained where it was, carved on the surface of the ball, spelling a name written in Arabic, Youssef -his brother's name. He stared at Abd Ana-eem, who, getting a little uncomfortable, shifted on his feet, and demanded, his voice distorted by strong-felt anxiety, "Did he say anything else?"

"No, nothing else…"

Noticing how uncomfortably looking his employee was, Khaled told him to go back to whatever he was doing. Once the young man had dashed out, the wood carver, shaking his head, made his way to the shelf, touched the other ball just to make sure it was actually there, palpable and real, and not an object he was imagining, perhaps because he had been working too hard, and hadn't eaten the whole day, as he happened to be fasting. Finding that it was definitely real, he sighed, walked to the workbench, and immediately away from it. He paced around and around, in and out of the shop, until he was so helplessly confused that he had to sit down, his eyes and mind completely under the spell of the wooden ball he was still holding, while in his head Abd An-eem's words came back, saying, over and over again, 'a carpenter, a very generous man…'

He remembered his brother, young and proud, caring and loving, a dreamer who wanted the best for himself and for his family. He remembered how the two of them cared for and stood by each other in times of need. And with that memory came guilt, in the form of a gnawing feeling that began hollowing his spirit out, and making him wish he had acted differently when he had once been given the opportunity, on that cursed day he could never forget.

On that blackened day, Khaled was riding his bicycle, running an errand for Haj Ali, when, and just as he turned at the corner of Farah Avenue, he saw his brother standing too close to a rich looking girl, holding her hand, his face too close to hers. He should have pedaled to where they were standing, and stopped the whole thing. He should have slapped his younger brother for dishonoring their father's name right there and then. He should have told Youssef to remember who he was, what honor meant, and what dishonor was, but he didn't he smirked, thought it alright, boys will be boys, and pedaled away, leaving his brother behind, to face the dire consequences of his actions on his own, to be broken by life and its unfairness. He never mentioned the incident, even when trouble arose, although by then, it was already too late. He could have changed everything, by acting as the eldest brother. He could have saved his family from so much grief. But he didn't.

Khaled walked back to his bench, put the ball in one of his denim trousers pockets, certain that it was the one he had once made and given to his brother, wondering if the carpenter, the generous man, was actually Youssef. The idea swirled in his head, slowly abating all the thoughts that had risen out of guilt and regret. He shook his head, thinking "Youssef, a carpenter, what an idea... and why not, he surely had a lot more talent than I did."

Khaled began grinning, as joy suddenly filled his heart. He reached for his chisel, took a deep breath, wondering about all the beautiful things he didn't know about his lost brother, and resumed his work, his spirit uplifted by the image of someone he missed, his dear brother, Youssef the trouble maker, the free spirit, living happily and in decency, and a carpenter of all things.

Yasmine is standing on wet sand, right at the edge of the Mediterranean, breathing heavily, when Andalou arrives next to her.

"Yasmine…" his heart is pounding rampantly.

She glares at him with burning eyes. He hasn't changed much, despite the six years that have passed, despite the new name, he is still the man she had loved and then hated, unconditionally and with all her heart. Her nostrils flare loathingly, as she turns her face to the sea.

He wants to speak, but can't. He searches for something, anything, to say, but finds himself overwhelmed by her agonizing breath, until he finally gives up, sighs and turns to face the sea.

They remain there, standing side by side, whirled in a storm of unheeding emotions, unaware of their surroundings, unaware of the sea's breath, and of the white and gray seagulls hovering in circles around the two of them. Too consumed by a rush of resurfacing memories, and a sleeping pain that was always there, waiting beneath the surface –to be reawakened and acknowledged again, they don't even notice Carlos, who's followed them and is now standing next to a capsized boat not too far behind them, nor do they sense the soft wind that is gently swirling around them..

Water stretches forth, and almost reaches their feet.

Yasmine watches the sand absorb it all, "You hurt me."

He turns to her, his shoulders sunken, "I'm sorry."

She shakes her head, "You ruined me."

"I didn't mean for it to be that way," his voice comes out despairingly broken.

"I've hated you for so long," she speaks dryly, "You left me with so much pain."

He looks away, "I've hated myself for that."

"Is that supposed to make me feel better?" She faces him, "All I wanted was to move on. I don't need this."

"I never stopped loving you Yasmine."

Yasmine cries, "Don't say that."

Tears distort his vision "I wish I had fought for us…"

"But you didn't. You pushed me away… I offered myself to you and you pushed me away."

"I would give my life to change what happened."

"It's too late."

"I… I'm sorry, Yasmine."

"I hate you, Youssef!" she shouts, "I hate you!"

He reaches for her hand, "I love you and I always will."

She pulls away and steps back, "How dare you?"

He lowers his arm, "I don't want to lie anymore."

She pleads, "What do you want from me?"

"I just want your forgiveness."

"How can I forgive you? I trusted you. I would have died for you had you asked me to."

"I was young… I had no way to provide, no way to protect my family…" He lowers his head, "Y-your parents… they would have never accepted me."

"I would have never let my parents, or anyone else, come between us. Do you hear me? Never!"

"I couldn't let my mother pay for our happiness…"

"What are you talking about?"

"Your mother… she found out about us…"

"What?"

Youssef shakes his head, "It doesn't matter anymore."

Yasmine glances at him, and swallows what tastes like bitterness, remembering what Paulo had said, 'Perhaps, he was as much of a victim as you were. Perhaps, the choice wasn't really his. And perhaps, his betrayal was an act of self-sacrifice inspired by love and care for you, by hopes of wonderful days to come.' She looks away.

Youssef hears her sobbing. He wants to reach and touch her, hold her, but is too afraid to move. So, he stares at his feet, with tears falling and disappearing in damp and porous sand. He closes his eyes and wipes his face with the back of his hand. When he opens them again, cool water touches his feet, allaying his confusion, while the wind is growing stronger at his back, almost pushing him to move a little closer to her.

He steps forward, "Why are you here?"

She shrugs, "I... don't know anymore," and pauses, annoyed by sand blown at her face, "This beach, and the boy... Carlos, they've been haunting me, in my dreams, for two years..."

He stares at her, puzzled, unable to immediately grasp what she is saying.

She spins around, "And you too. You're the silhouette in the dark, behind the boy." Crossing her arms in front of her chest, she continues, "You, the boy, this place, you all appear, again and again, night after night, at four in the morning, no matter what I try..."

Youssef stammers, bewildered by what he's heard, "Every morning, Carlos and I walk out to stand in front of your picture." He takes a deep breath and explains, "Carlos prays to keep hope in his heart," and extends his arm, offering his palm, "and I pray for you to be well; to be happy."

She looks at his hand and sniffles, anger receding from her face, and softness setting in her heart.

Strands of hair reach for him, as the wind swirls faster, "Why are you here? Why draw me?"

Youssef steps closer, "I am here to keep a promise I made to a friend. I promised him to take care of his wife and of his son, if his time were to come while we were at sea. I promised him that I would build a shop and paint something from the heart on the wall facing the sea."

He looks at the building and sees Carlos, standing between Esperanza and them. He smiles and continues, "I stood in front of that wall for a year, not knowing what to paint," his dimples appear shyly, "then, an old man passed by. He stopped to ask for some water. I invited him to share a meal."

Yasmine melts inside, as the dimples deepen. The past floods her mind, overwhelming her ability to think, and in the midst of that storm of images from a life she'd done her best to forget, appears the face of that old man who comes in for a meal; Paulo Aduro.

Youssef continues, "He asked me about the wall. I told him my story and that I couldn't decide what to paint. He looked at me, as if knowing everything about me, as if he were able to see what I held deep within me. Then, he advised me to listen to my heart, to let it guide my hand. He told me to express what was undoubtedly true to me."

Yasmine looks at the painting, looks at herself, the way she had once been, when her heart was full to brim with nothing but love.

Youssef wipes his face again, laughs, tears still falling, and continues, "So I listened to my heart, and when I did, all I could hear was your voice. When I closed my eyes, all I could see was you." He reaches for her hand and touches it, explaining, "You are the one I found in my heart."

Yasmine steps closer, arguing, "I'm married now, whatever was between us..." and remembers the last words he had told her, six years ago.

Youssef brings her palm against his chest, "What is between us can never be over." He takes a deep breath, "I love you Yasmine."

Yasmine tenses, as too many reasons to hate him flash in her head, the past with all of its pain and disappointments weighing heavily against her battered soul. For so long, she's wanted to see him in agony. She's wanted justice. She'd wanted explanations.

But, upon looking into his eyes, all of her tension, anger, and wants feel as unbearable as an outer shell she is ready to outgrow, a fortress she no longer needs.

"I love you," cries Youssef.

"I..." she draws closer, almost tasting his breath, her eyes lost in the tenderness she can recognize in his, "I love you too Youssef. God, I love you too." The shell disintegrates and the fortress crumbles to be blown away like dust caught in the wind.

Water reaches them. The circling wind intensifies, yet when it touches them, it feels like a soft caress meant to dry out their tears.

They embrace, tightly wrapping their arms around each other, responding to the voice of love and satisfying a need for closeness that would no longer be denied. They embrace, and meld in the intensity of the moment; chest pressing against chest, hearts flooded with passion, reason and fear silenced. They surrender and let their lips touch, igniting fires they had forgotten existed in their hearts.

In the distance, the villagers cover their eyes, to protect themselves from the gusting wind, and thus fail to witness two loving souls, rekindled by passion, spiraling to the sky, sheltered in swirling veils of sand.

When the wind dies out, it leaves all those who witnessed its passing brimming with an overwhelming feeling of serenity that can be seen shining through their faces, as they stand staring in bewilderment at Esperanza, Andalou and Carlos who are heading back to the village.

The following morning, a pleasant wind blowing south, across the sea, connecting one continent to another, meets an old man walking along an empty road in Tangier. The man stops, closes his eyes and smiles contently.

A few moments later, in Casablanca, a grandmother, busily bent over her sewing table, her eyes focused behind corrective lenses, is interrupted by a little boy's appearance, as he slams the door of her modest seamstress shop and sprints in her direction to give her a loving hug, followed by a cool breeze that brings every piece of fabric it passes to life.

The grandmother holds her little angel, and, while smiling at the dancing strips and sheets of colorful fabrics. Acknowledging the wind caressing her face, she smiles and closes her eyes, feeling touched by love, and experiencing undeniable peace.

At that exact moment, a doctor and his assistant, in love, wrapped under the softness of white linen sheets, hidden from the world, behind the thick walls of a modern apartment, a doubly locked door and a closed window, are bathing in morning light.

By the window, outside, a tree sways rhythmically, chanting along with the wind. Its hushed melody leaks into the room, where its soothing sound is taken as a blessing to undo what is wrong, to follow one's heart into complete submission to the other -the lover, the partner, the soul mate. Today a seed is planted, as they both embrace, with closed eyes and open hearts, nestled in the whisper of a singing tree, their minds lost in the sweetness of hopes and dreams.

"Hello, Mom?" Yasmine, standing in front of an oval-shaped public phone box, presses her ear against the receiver.

"I'm still in Spain…" She looks at Youssef and Carlos leaning on the parked rental car, both holding a guitar, playing and laughing.

"I know… I know…Listen. I just spoke to Adil. Mom, can you hear me? We're getting divorced."

She smiles nervously, as she watches Youssef holding and playing notes from a Gypsy song, amazed at how much better he had gotten since those old days when she patiently tried teaching him how to play.

She grins, watching Youssef's fingers softly stroking the strings of the guitar he has offered her, and says, "Do you remember when I dreamed of traveling all over the world and singing about love, for anyone in love, for anyone loved? Maybe, it's not too late for that."

Anxiously, she rocks on her feet, "Mother, please… It's our decision."

Examining his face, she finds all that she had been missing, and shakes her head, almost disbelieving that she's finally decided to be true to herself, and follow her heart, wherever her heart may take her.

"I don't know… In a couple of weeks…No, I really don't know… I guess work will have to wait."

Looking at the boy, she sees a son she has dreamed of having, for so many years. Watching him play and laugh, she experiences unconditional love and comes to peace with her body's inability to procreate.

She waves at Youssef who winks at her, "Nothing… Nothing is going on… It's complicated. I'll tell you when

I get back." She looks at both of them, and sees home and family.

"I sound happy?" she sighs, feeling relieved

"Yes, I guess I am happy," she chuckles.

Yasmine pulls a car key out of her pocket, "Mom, I have to go... Mom... I love you... Yes... Bye."

Youssef and Carlos watch her as she hangs up and runs back to the car. They all hug, climb in: Carlos in the back, Yasmine behind the wheel, and Youssef next to her. She leans over and kisses Youssef, turns the ignition key and starts the engine. The roof is down, the road's empty, and the sky's perfectly clear.

Carlos, head turned to the road behind them, watches the phone booth as it is swallowed by the vacuum of speed. He watches it disappear, along with that melancholy he's been carrying ever since his mother left him. Turning around, he finds Andalou and Esperanza. Carlos grins, because within their binding love he feels safe, whatever the road ahead and the future may bring.